MW01482272

Heart Land

A Place Called 'Ockley Green'

By Caroline Miller

Koho Pono
Novel

Heart Land: A Place Called 'Ockley Green'
Published by Koho Pono, LLC
Clackamas, Oregon USA
http://KohoPono.com

For general information on our other products, please contact our
Customer Service Department within the USA at 503-723-7392 or
visit http://KohoPono.com.

Second Edition 10march2015

ISBN: 978-1-938282-16-4 - Paperback
ISBN: 978-1-938282-17-1 - EBook

What reviewers say about Caroline Miller's books:

"Both novels [*Gothic Spring* and *Heart Land*] combine the energy and creativity of Miller's youth and sagacious wisdom of a woman who has seen the world and experienced first-hand progressive change."

> *- SE Examiner, October 2009*

"Ms. Miller is a powerful, eloquent writer."

> *– Silver Reviews*

"When looking back is looking forward - *Heart Land* is sweet, deft and subtle... Sometimes funny, occasionally poignant, *Heart Land* is a first-rate, observant look at prewar life in a small Ohio town. It is a time and place that are mythic now. Honesty, courage, and caring, friends, relatives, family and community are linked in generational and geographic semi-isolation, and every one knows and (mostly) cares about everybody else. Adults try to understand, children struggle to live up to adult values, and small incidents loom large as major life lessons are drawn from them.

Integrity and compassion underlie *Heart Land*'s sensibility. Its people are real living, breathing human beings. Miller's work is engaging; an often lyric expression of small-town Midwestern America left not so long behind, with solid, reliable echoes that still lead to a simple, but well justified life."

> *– John Legry, author of* The Copper-Handles Affair

"... *Heart Land* wears the triple crown of literary genius: it is profound, beautiful and arresting from the first page..."

> *– Writerface.com, the online social network for writers & literary agents*

"... a beautifully scripted tale of two boys and their unforgettable home town."

– Leigh Goodison, author of <u>WildOnes</u>

Dedication

In memory of my dear friends: Oliver and Vivian Larson.

Acknowledgements

I wish to acknowledge the wonderful work of Leona Grieve who served as my personal editor in helping me to pull this book together.

I wish to thank Anne Koch for her kind permission to use excerpts from 'The War of the Worlds', 1938 radio dramatization, in my Chapter *VI - Of Ghosts, Goblins, and Little Green Men.*

Contents

Prologue

The snow crunched under my feet as I climbed the wooden stairs of the craftsman house that had been the family home since Mom and Dad were married. The grey stone siding looked indestructible but the numerous windows, most of them blinded by drapes pulled tightly across, spoke of the sadness within. I shifted the weight of the groceries I was carrying to my left hip and used my right hand to turn the brass handle of the front door. It opened easily, the familiar creak still present as I stepped over the threshold.

"I'm back," I called to the empty hall and headed for the kitchen.

Herman, my younger brother of about four years, answered back. "We're in the living room. I've started a fire. Dad didn't notice but it's getting cold in here."

"Great." I tossed the words over my shoulder as I crossed the dining room, still headed for the kitchen. Once there, I unloaded my groceries, dropped the potatoes into the sink for scrubbing and placed the steaks in the refrigerator until it was time to put them under the broiler.

The menu, though simple, represents the extent of my culinary skills. Too often, my days were spent eating in cheap hotels and only then when I was lucky, The other times, I'd be chowing down on military rations with a platoon of U.S. soldiers somewhere in Vietnam and worrying about flying bullets that didn't make a distinction between men who carried guns and men who carried pads of paper and pencils. As a foreign correspondent, a man in his early forties, I was too old to fight this war but young enough to record it.

My wife hates my job because it can be dangerous and often takes me half way across the globe. In spite of the obstacles, we managed to have two beautiful daughters.

Yesterday, I put the three of them on a plane back to our home in San Francisco, as I'd decided to stay on in Ohio to help Dad settle Mom's affairs. Her funeral was three days ago.

When I entered the living room Dad was seated in his overstuffed chair, the velveteen arms worn to a nub despite the doilies Mom had placed there to protect them. He didn't look up, but continued to stare into the fire, not even blinking as I crossed in front of him to occupy the chair opposite. Herman, seated on a stool by the hearth, looked up and gave me a smile.

"I thought we'd have steak for dinner," I announced.

Dad remained silent at first, then grunted his approval.

"I didn't buy any rolls," I went on. "The equivalent of Mom's biscuits can't be bought at any store, but we've got bread."

Dad nodded a second time, but with his right hand, he covered his eyes. The slightest reference to his wife of 41 years cut through him like a carving knife.

I winced at my stupidity. Mom had died suddenly of a brain aneurysm. He'd had no time to prepare.

The whole community was shocked by her passing. No one thought of our parents as anything but robust. Dad at the age of 62 still worked as a policeman and with his trim appearance and iron grey hair, he cut a handsome figure. Mom remained petite all her life and the week before she died, she'd signed up at the library to read to the children during story hour. Next summer, 1971, she and Dad planned a trip to San Francisco to stay with my family.

Herman hadn't given them any grandchildren yet. He was too busy making money as a stock broker in Columbus. But he and his wife, Ariste, both of them addicted to planning everything, had promised that by next summer a third grandchild would be in the works.

Conversation was light at the supper table. I talked a little about my experiences in Vietnam. Dad listened with his head bowed, his eyes boring steadily into his plate. "Too many wars," he whispered as if to himself. "Too many good people lost."

Herman and I stared across the table at one another. We knew Dad was thinking of his brother, Tom, and his in-law, Uncle Henry. Both of them were killed in World War II. We almost lost Mom then to grief.

After the meal, Dad went upstairs to rest while Herman and I cleared up in the kitchen. We fell into an easy rhythm with me washing and my brother drying. For a while the years fell away and we were kids again.

"Dad's sleeping a lot," Herman observed after an interval of silence. "Do you think he should have a check up?"

"Naw. Leave him alone. The sleep's doing him good. It's the only place where he can find peace."

"I suppose so." Herman looked doubtful. He was always one to want to make things better. I admired him for his spirit, especially when the trail of broken shards that constituted the landscape of my life didn't always leave me hopeful. That's the curse of being a war correspondent, I suppose.

"This old town sure is funny," I said, trying to turn Herman's mind away from worrying about our dad. "So much has changed and yet in some ways, things seem the same."

Herman, now in his late thirties, nodded. "Yeah, I suppose the change is more dramatic for you, having been away so long. I get down from Columbus every two or three months. We've got a high school now, in case you haven't seen it. Remember Homer Nordling's cornfield? That's where they built it. The town's grown enough so that the kids don't have to be bussed to Goshen anymore. We've even got our own baseball team."

"We?" You sound like you still live here."

My brother lowered his head, embarrassed by my observation. "Yeah, well, you know. . . with you overseas so much, someone has to..."

"It hasn't been easy for me, if that's what you think. I'd like to be here more, but I've got a family in San Francisco. God knows, I see them little enough. Sometimes when I get home from assignment, I don't even recognize my own kids waiting for me at the airport."

Herman cleared his throat by way of an apology. "I didn't mean anything by what I said, Ollie. You've done your part. You've sent money -- which Dad refused to take, by the way. Mom had me invest it secretly, though; so he doesn't have any financial worries. He can buy a fleet of Cadillacs if he wants."

Remembering our dad's abhorrence of automobiles, I had to laugh. Mostly, he walked his beat, which probably accounted for his good health.

"I see the old elementary school is still going." I wanted to give another turn to the conversation. "Looks like they've put an extension on it."

"Yeah, they did. The freeway may have passed us by but there's been growth. People keep moving to the 'suburbs' and buying up the land. Aren't many farms around anymore. There's even a mini mall on the west end of town. The new folks shop there but the natives stick to their old haunts."

"And the Marabar Diner? That's got a new name. Thanh Thao? A Thai restaurant?"

"Oscar sold out when his arthritis got too bad. He lives in Arizona now. The food's pretty good under the new management. Not something I'd want to eat everyday, but it makes for a change. I miss Oscar's coffee, though. Remember how good it was?"

Herman and I stood in companionable silence, remembering the rich, fudge-like aroma of Oscar's brew, a treat forbidden to us as kids because Dad was certain it would stunt our growth.

"But the library's the same." My brother, who was two inches shorter than I, grinned up at me.

He assumed I'd given a wide berth to the place, but he was wrong about that. Years before, under the withering glances of Miss Berenson, the librarian, a hobo and I had passed a memorable afternoon together. In that cosseted space with its stucco walls and high beamed ceilings, he'd opened my eyes to the magic of books and that memory burned as brightly as if it were yesterday.

"Except for the history books," Herman went on. "They're at Hettie Maitland's place. The Victorian's been turned into a community hall of sorts. People can rent it for receptions or special events, and the historical society gives tours on Saturdays to anyone who signs up. I always thought opening her house to the public was a great idea. Hettie loved having people underfoot. I bet she's up in the clouds somewhere, smiling."

"I wouldn't doubt it," I said, handing my brother the broiling pan that I'd wiped clear of grease.

As we were near the end of our chores, Herman asked the question that I was certain had been perched on the end of his tongue. "How long do you think you can stay with us, Ollie? Dad's gonna need help sorting through things, and I could use the company. So many of the neighbors who'd have pitched in are gone."

You know Mr. and Mrs. Katafias have passed on. Mr. Papadopoulos owns their property next door, but he's still doing concerts. He's only here in the summer and fall. And I wrote you about the Hjalmers. They've moved to Colorado to be near their daughter and grandchildren. Their son-in-law bought them a condominium. Who'd ever guess he'd make a success as a banker?" Herman stared into his damp dishtowel, his thoughts drifting. "So much has changed."

"That's inevitable." I shrugged.

He didn't seem to hear me. "Miss Ingrid's retired. Some fella from New York bought her Bake Shoppe and turned it into a catering establishment. Mr. Swanson hangs around the hardware store but his son runs the business."

"What about the Criterion?" I tried to sound cheerful. "It's still going."

"Yeah, it's around. Mostly, it shows old movies. It can't compete with the big screen theatre at the new mall."

"Any chance we might catch one of those old Lash LaRue serials?"

Herman laughed his whole face crinkling. "Naw, they're too old even for the Criterion." After that my brother turned silent again, his unanswered question hanging between us.

"I'll stay with you and Dad as long as I can, Herman," I said at last. "But there's a war going on..."

My brother shook his head. "Yeah, I know. There always seems to be a war going on. But you don't have to be in this one, do you? Couldn't you get a job back in San Francisco? I worry about you, Bro. I worry that one of these days, you'll come home in a body bag. And for what? A by-line?"

"Have you forgotten I've got a family to feed?"

"No, I haven't forgotten. You married Nancy Gunderson, the girl you fell in love with in the sixth grade. And now you've got two beautiful girls that look just like her. Have you wondered what would happen to them if you didn't come home one day? And what about Dad and Aunt Enid and the rest of us. How do you think we'd feel?" The bitterness in my brother's voice surprised me. "I thought you supported this war."

Herman looked up with a crease in his forehead. "Hell no. Where'd you get that idea?"

"Didn't you write that you'd like to see all the flower children planted in foxholes?"

"Yes. But that's because I don't think the burden of this war is being shared by everyone. Going to college or running off to Canada shouldn't get a person a free pass."

"Okay, maybe you're right and the flower children are wrong. How does that affect me? I'm over there, aren't I?"

"But you don't have to be. That's the point."

"You can't have it both ways, Herman. Either we share the burden or we don't."

"Damn it, Ollie, you always could argue circles around me."

"That's because I'm older, Bro."

Herman didn't say anything after that, but I could feel his eyes on me as I wiped the counter clean and helped him put the dishes away in the cupboard. Finally, I took pity on him. "I'll stay as long as you need me. At least until we've sorted through Mom's things and get Dad squared away. Okay?"

"Okay, Ollie." My brother spoke barely above a whisper. "But promise me, when you go back, you'll take care of yourself, won't ya?"

"I'll even eat my broccoli."

After breakfast the next morning, Dad announced that he was going for a walk. He'd been holed up in the house since the funeral, but his decision didn't surprise Herman or me. We knew he couldn't bear to hang around while I boxed up Mom's personal belongings.

"Shall I come with you, Dad?" Herman's eyes were uplifted like a dog begging to tag along.

"I'll only be gone an hour," Dad grunted. "Less if it's too cold."

Herman knew an hour wouldn't give me much time. "Why don't we walk to the park? Hettie's place will be open and we could have some coffee and a slice of her poppy seed cake. It's not as good as her original recipe -- Hettie would never share that -- but it's pretty good. On the way back we can stop at the hardware store. I'd like to pick up a snow shovel for you. The one you've got's dented."

"It works well enough."

"I know, but I'd like to replace it for you. Some of the new ones are easier on your back."

"Nothing's wrong with my back."

"Maybe so, but we're all growing older. I'm thinking of buying one for myself."

"Do it then. But I don't need a new shovel."

Herman put one arm around our father's shoulder. "Come on. Humor me will you? "

Dad headed for the door without answering.

"It's cold outside," Herman called after him. "Where're your gloves? Have you got 'em with you?"

Dad pulled his gloves from his pocket and waved them in the air. "I'm not old and I'm not senile. Now are you coming?"

Herman mouthed back at me as he closed the front door, "I'll try to keep him out as long as I can."

Turning the knob of my parent's bedroom was an action I took slowly, reverently. When I was a toddler I'd bounded in and out at will. But as I grew older, I'd learned to respect Mom and Dad's privacy. Entering now, I felt more like a voyeur than a member of the family.

Mom's dresser stood by a window across the room. How many times I'd seen her sitting before it, that kidney shaped table with its mirror suspended on a wooden frame, I don't know, but I'd always admired its carved grace and the hand painted roses that seemed to blossom from their cream colored background. Perhaps Nancy or one of the girls might like to have it?

The moment the thought crossed my mind, I blushed, feeling ashamed. Now was not the time to think of disposition. To leave the room with so much space would underscore my mother's absence.

As to the dresser's contents, mercifully they would not be so easily missed: the Ponds Cold Cream and the bottle of Jergens lotion with which she used to slather her face, neck and arms. These I tossed without remorse into one of the paper bags I'd carried up with me. But when my hand fell upon a little perfume bottle, to my surprise, I pulled it back, instantly.

I could almost hear my mother chiding me. "Not the Tabu, Oliver. Not after all these years." And she would be right. That empty bottle was too full of memories to discard. I slipped it into my pants pocket, instead, uncertain of my intentions.

Clearing the two drawers on either side of the mirror took little time. In one I found a few dime store lipsticks. In the other there were bobby pins and curlers. Mom hadn't needed much feminine paraphernalia. She was a beautiful woman inside as well as out.

Her clothes and her few pieces of costume jewelry were destined to be packed into boxes and sent to the church. They would be disposed of at a rummage sale and the money used for charity. Countless women before her had made the same bequest, confident that their final gift would be treated with reverence by the friends they'd left behind. So it was when I was a boy. So it would be far into the future.

The closet revealed the same symmetry and order that Mom had given to our lives. Dad's suits hung on the right, together with his ties. Her dresses formed a colorful row on the left. On the floor stretched a serpentine line of shoes. As expected, Dad's were on the right: one pair of work shoes, one pair of dress shoes and one pair of boots. The remaining space was dominated by ladies footwear, size 5 double A.

As I reached down to begin clearing her items away, I came across a stack of photo albums tucked into a far corner of the space. It seemed a peculiar place to store albums, so I pulled them out and stacked them on my parent's bed. Each was labeled by year, some of them going so far back that their contents were yellow with age. Oddly enough the later books had received less attention than the earlier ones. Their pictures had not been affixed to the pages but tossed among them as if waiting for a time when they would receive my mother's attention. That time never came. Once her children moved away, Mom seemed to have lost interest in her project.

Seating myself in the rocker that stood beside the bed, I began to turn the pages of the fattest album, the one marked "1939-1940." Herman was 7 at the time and I was almost 12. So many memories came flooding back to me.

If the years of one's life could be categorized like wine, I'd say that 1939 was a vintage year, a breathing space between the hardships of the Depression and the looming despair of World War II. But, of course, I didn't realize how good life was in those days. I was a kid growing up in a small, mostly rural farming community in Ohio -- a place where the resident's were kind and eccentricities were tolerated... a place called Ockley Green.

Chapter 1 - The Summer of the Burlap Bag

Photograph: *Oliver, petting Bodacious Scurvy with Mrs. Katafias looking on, June, 1939*

Recollections about my youth tend to begin with the summer of 1939, the summer Bodacious Scurvy tangled with the burlap bag. Bodacious was an alley cat, probably the orneriest and weirdest looking animal to swagger through the tall Ohio grass. He looked like a cross between a Persian and a Siamese. His body was a sleek black, except for the head and tail both of which flared at the sides, especially when Bodacious Scurvy was unhappy.

Calling him "Scurvy" was my idea on account of his ragged looks. The tag, "Bodacious" came later when our neighbor, Mrs. Katafias, took to feeding him and addressing him as such. She had never laid any claim to him because Mr. Katafias was allergic to cats.

If allergies had been the only trait to define Mr. Katafias, I suspect that summer would not have been so memorable. But it wasn't. For one thing, he was an herbalist, a fact which we narrow-minded boys from a small town transformed into a mystery. Witchdoctor, that's how we thought of him, especially when we caught him prowling in the woods behind the school. Under the shadows of the trees he seemed a sinister figure, bent over the grass and shrubs, and mumbling words in a foreign tongue which we were certain was a spell. "Greek," that's what my mother said it was, but magic described it better.

1

My fascination with Mr. Katafias was fixed by a remark dropped by my father to Mom one afternoon while she was making preserves in the kitchen. He was a policeman, a trained observer, and so I put a lot of store in what he said.

"Scoff if you want to, Elsie. But the days of Bodacious Scurvy are numbered."

"That's nonsense, John Larson, and you know it." She laughed. "You're just like the boys. Always looking for a reason to fault Mr. Katafias. What's the poor man ever done to you?"

"Nothing. Guess you've never seen him react whenever that cat crosses his path." Dad was settling down to his onion sandwich. "The old man goes white as a sheet."

Mom stared at dad as if he was crazy. After that, the conversation turned to talk of Uncle Henry, my mother's brother who lived with us, a man whom some folks thought was strange, too. My mother said he acted different from everybody else because he was sensitive.

My dad said it was because he was a 'no-account bum.' He didn't say this often, though, because it made my mother's cheeks go red.

That conversation in the kitchen planted an idea in my head, which I decided to share with my kid brother, he being seven and me almost twelve. "Lash," I began. (When we were alone, he refused to answer to 'Herman' and called himself Lash LaRue.) "Do you think that Mr. Katafias believes in ghosts?"

Lash stared at me, wondering what I was up to. I admit he had reason to be suspicious because I'd often made him the butt of one of my beautiful jokes. But this time, he could see I was sincere.

"Yep," he said, after some consideration. "It's possible, I

reckon."

I told him I had a plan to find out and Lash admitted my idea was worthy of further consideration.

Our chance to put that plan into action came when Mrs. Katafias was called away to attend to a sick aunt in Duluth. It was nearly five o'clock on a Saturday afternoon when Mr. Katafias returned from the bus station, after seeing his wife off. That's when Lash and I hightailed it over to his house on the pretext of needing a cup of sugar.

Mr. Katafias never questioned our errand and led us into the kitchen. There's where we dropped hints about an 'Injun' burial ground being in his cellar.

"Injun burial ground?" Mr. Katafias' eyes grew round as he poured the sugar from its sack, allowing it to overflow the cup and spill in rivulets on the counter. My little brother and I winked at one another.

"Yep," Herman went on. "There must be a hundred of spirits lyin' right here, under this kitchen. Massacreed they was by Custer hisself!"

By now the sack of sugar was almost empty. Its contents, having breached the drain board, formed snowy peaks upon the floor.

"Th-th-i-s true?" asked Mr. Katafias, casting a crazed glance in my direction.

I answered him solemnly, as if I were under oath. "Oh, it's true all right. And I've got to say, you're a brave man, sir. Awful brave. Any night those spirits could rise up and take their revenge upon the unsuspecting living. I'd hate to be around here, if they did. Yes sir, Mr. Katafias. I expect you're just about the bravest man I know."

My brother nodded slowly, as if his head were attached to a rusty hinge. Mr. Katafias continued to look uneasy. He followed us out the door, watching as we descended his porch steps, like a man hoping for an invitation to come home with us. By then he was pale enough to be one of those ghosts we'd been going on about. Lash and I didn't dare look at one another to keep from splitting our sides.

"That was great! That was great!" My brother danced in front of me once we'd rounded the corner. "He took the bait, hook, line and sinker! You're a genius, Oliver. Ya know that?"

"Aw, it's nothing." I shrugged, trying to sound casual. "Wait and see what happens next!"

Lash stopped dancing; his mouth hung open. "What do ya mean? What's next?"

As I had no idea at the time, I broke off into a run. "Come on, nosey. Last one home has to set table."

At midnight, the hall clock tolled the hour with a slow and heavy beat, a sound I usually wasn't awake to hear. But that night, I'd been staring at the ceiling, thinking. Outside, nothing stirred, not even the leaves on the sycamore. It was another quiet summer night in our small town. Through the curtains, the moon silvered a wedge across my brother's pillow.

He was in a dead sleep, snoring a little.

"Lash," I called out to him. "Lash, it's midnight." No answer, just that same little puttering noise as before. A second and third time I tried to wake him, but with no effect. Knowing our mother was a light sleeper, I decided to crawl out of bed and shake him. "Criminetly!" I whispered, "The night's half over! Wake up, will ya!"

A pair of eyes snapped open. A body bolted upright. With his hair spiking at right angles from his head, Lash looked ready for a fight. "Wh-What is it? What's the matter? Uncle Henry had another nightmare?"

"It's midnight! Time to get up!"

Lash looked at me like I was crazy enough to chew ground glass just for the pleasure of it. "Get up? What for?"

"Time for the Injun gho-s-sts!" I sniggered, flicking my fingers above his head. For a moment, he remained stupefied, but when he got the idea, his face soured.

"Aw for crumb sakes. I ain't gettin' out of bed now. Tomorrow we'll do something. After breakfast."

When I heard him, I could hardly believe my ears. "Are you crazy? Ghosts don't rise from the grave after breakfast! They need the dark so their spirits show. So they can SCARE people."

"Says you!"

"Yeah, says me! I read all about it somewhere."

"You never read nothin'," my brother snorted confidently. "Mama says you're just like Uncle Henry. Got no interest in ed-ja-cation! Day dreaming is all you do. Anyway, we're not talkin' about real ghosts. There ain't no Injuns buried under Mr. Katafias' kitchen and Custer was never anywhere near here."

"But Mr. Katafias don't know that!" I reminded him.

"Yeah and Mr. Katafias don't know that ghosts need the dark to show their selves neither. Morning ghosts is just as good!" And with that, Lash pulled the covers over his head and refused to answer to another word I said, not even when I called him, "HER-MAN!"

Disgusted, I threatened to leave him. "I'll do it myself, then. I don't need you! Just don't come cryin' to me when you miss out on all the fun!"

At the window, I paused for any sign of a change of heart. There was none. The lump in my brother's bed was as still as a grave site. I was forced to hit the cool grass below our window with only my shirttails for company.

Finding Bodacious Scurvy, as I'd hoped, was not hard. He was curled up on the back porch of the Katafias household on some old clothes that Mrs. Katafias had piled up to make a bed for him. He eyed me warily as I approached. The last time our paths had crossed, I'd scared him up a sycamore with a lighted firecracker. Bodacious had a long memory and could hold a grudge.

On such a hot night, however, he was reluctant to move, though he looked suspicious when I bent down to scratch behind his ear. He didn't purr either. Purring was beneath him; but he kept his eye on me all the same. Me and the burlap bag I was carrying.

Once I'd decided the cat would stay put, I crept into the house.

People never locked their doors in our community as crime was practically unknown -- something that only happened to people foolish enough to live in a city. At least, that's what my dad said.

Heading for the kitchen in my bare feet, I tramped like an army on the march. A pan had been left unwashed on the counter. This I dropped with an admirable thud. It rolled around a second or two and made a sort of growl. If there'd been any dead people buried in the cellar, by now they were wide awake. But the dead weren't who I was after.

Overhead, I heard some bed springs creak. The time had come

for my final and best effect. "W-wo-o-o... W-wo-o-o." The sound echoed in the kitchen and, like smoke, floated to the top of the stairs. In my mind's eye, I imagined Mr. Katafias sitting bolt upright in his bed, his hands clutching at his sheets. I couldn't stop chortling as I fled from the house.

Bodacious, still on his pile of rags, growled when he saw me. He hadn't time for much else because with a magician's slight of hand, I scooped him up and hurled him into the burlap bag. He was yowling loud enough to shatter glass as I tossed the bundle into the root cellar.

By the time I'd reached the sycamore outside my bedroom, lights were on all over the neighborhood. Someone complained to the night air, "I'll bet it's that Uncle Henry having one of his nightmares again!"

By noon the next day, news of the disturbance was all over town. Apparently, someone had called the police and when they found Bodacious Scurvy balled up in the root cellar, one outraged neighbor came forward to say that he knew for a fact that Katafias had it in for that stray. This wasn't the first time there'd been a skirmish between the two.

Another neighbor, among those who had gathered, pointed to the scratches on the old man's arms. They spoke, he said, to the truth about the feud between man and cat. Lastly, someone in the crowd was heard to murmur, "One never knows about these foreigners. They don't think like the rest of us."

Nobody believed the old man's story that there were mummies buried in his root cellar. He was fined three dollars for disturbing the peace and ordered to stay clear of the cat. Disgruntled, Mr. Katafias retreated into his house, slamming the screen door as a protest of his innocence.

Around midnight of the following evening, I returned to the Katafias' house. Bodacious spied me and took off in flash. I was prepared for that and had come with a set of my own noisemakers: a bike chain and some sleigh bells. The back door remained unlocked, as I'd expected. Mr. Katafias, of all people, wouldn't attempt to lock out a ghost.

Tiptoeing into the kitchen, I laid out my instruments on the empty counter. I was careful to make no noise until everything was arranged. Then I broke into a crude rendition of Jingle Bells.

The unseasonable tinkling had its effect. A light flashed on at the top of the stairs. A pair of soft slippers began their descent. With no time for the chorus, I raced toward the back door. My bike chain lay forgotten in the kitchen sink, but I managed a "W-w-o-o-o, w-o-o-o" before disappearing into the night.

The audacity of my third haunting surprised even me. But I was too full of myself to question a door that was not only unlocked but slightly ajar. My hand pressed against it with a light touch, the kind one might use to wake a sleeping baby, but it was powerful enough to change my life.

A pail had been balanced overhead and at my touch, it toppled to the floor with crash. Startled, I let out a yowl that would have made Bodacious Scurvy proud. But the pail was the least of my troubles. Its contents, a gooey substance, had been deposited on top of my head. It was oozing into my eyes and ears and no amount of rubbing could wipe it away. The condition grew worse. In no time, I would be deaf as well as blind. Terrified, I hurled myself off the Katafias' porch and headed for home, trusting my feet to know the way.

Herman bounced me awake the next morning. He was sitting at the side of my bed as I pried my eyes open. Apparently, I hadn't succeeded in wiping away all the goop of the night before. But I could hear him plainly enough. He was laughing so hard that he broke into hiccups.

"(Hic) Maybe you should run away to the circus! Yeah, you could be a clown! (Hic) Or one of those sideshow freaks! (Hic, Hic.)

"Suck eggs!" I hissed as I leapt out of bed. I wasn't in the mood to play games with my brother. I needed to know what had set him off, though. Downstairs, I could hear Uncle Henry and my parents talking. That meant the bathroom was free. I sprinted across the hall and locked the door behind me so Herman couldn't follow.

As my feet turned cold on the tile floor, I stared into the mirror over the sink. The face gazing back at me was that of a Martian or something from outer space. But when I swiveled my head to the right, the face in the mirror swiveled also. And that was my hand exploring the green chin, the green forehead. Those were my fingers combing through hair that was the color of grass.

"What in tar nations?" I cried.

I reached for my wash cloth and lathered my face until I foamed at the mouth like a rabid dog. Five minutes of scrubbing went by and then ten, but the image in the mirror hadn't altered. If it'd been Halloween, I'd have made a great bean stalk. But as it was summer, the only place to blend in would be among the water lilies in Mrs. Katafias's garden.

By now my little brother, his mouth like a megaphone, was broadcasting the details of my condition to the folks in the kitchen. Mom came rushing to the top of the stairs to pound on the bathroom door.

"Oliver? Herman says you're green! What have you been up to? Are you sick?"

"No Mom. I'm fine."

"Then open this door. Now!"

Mom jiggled the handle, her voice a mixture of annoyance and alarm. I didn't have time to concoct a story. What I needed was a miracle. My eyes rolled up to the ceiling in the hope of finding one there. That's when I heard it, an angel's voice.

"Elsie? Are you upstairs? May I speak to you a moment?"

Mom let go of the door knob. In the silence, I supposed she was deciding how to answer the question. On the one hand, she was determined to discover my mischief; on the other, she couldn't be rude to a guest. Finally, she hissed through the door. "Go to your room, Oliver, and wait for me!" Then she hurried downstairs to greet Mrs. Katafias.

In bed, with the covers pulled up to my chin, I stared into space, hoping a fib might come to me. Maybe I could blame my condition on last night's broccoli. Maybe I could say I had an allergy. Yeah, that was a great idea. I was allergic to broccoli and maybe spinach, too, and asparagus.

I was almost smiling when Mom and Mrs. Katafias entered my room. They were giving one another sidelong glances as if they shared a secret.

"It's all right, Oliver," Mom said, placing a cool hand on my forehead. "Mrs. Katafias knows all about your condition. She's brought some medicine to ease the pain."

Pain? The roots of my hair snapped to attention.

The old woman, her head wrapped in a kerchief, gave me a thin smile. "Yes, yes. I've seen this a few times in the old country. But not in one so young." Then she shook her head, as if to suggest my condition might be fatal.

Now it was her turn to place a hand upon my forehead. "No fever, yet. That's a good sign. But you must be faithful to my remedy, young man.

10

Otherwise..." She shrugged and threw up her hands. "Otherwise, only God knows your fate."

Staring up at the women, I was as confused as a dog between two fire hydrants. I knew I was green, but I was feeling all right. Surely Mrs. Katafias knew that, too. She had to be the one who'd set the trap above her door. Mr. Katafias wouldn't cotton to schemes.

Any doubts about our neighbor's intentions were dispelled when she tossed the burlap bag she'd been hiding on to my bed. I recognized it at once by the holes Bodacious Scurvy had inflicted upon it in his struggle to get free.

Mrs. Katafias gave me a second thin smile as she reached into the bag. "You must drink six times a day for three days," she said, pulling out a bottle and placing the stopper under my nose.

I pushed her hand away without thinking. What assailed my senses was a brew akin to a fermented outhouse. Still, I'd have been blessed if that were my only torture. Next, she placed a yoke of garlic about my neck and told me to wear it. The herb was bad enough but it was garlanded in ribbons, adding insult to injury.

I'd had enough and started to rise, but the old woman held me down with a strength I'd never imagined. "Three days from today. Not a moment before," she went on, holding up what looked like a bottle of bath salts. "Bathe in this."

As expected, my little brother took advantage of my predicament. Every slight I'd paid him in his young life came back to haunt me. What's more, he'd found a way to make money from his revenge. By the end of my first day's imprisonment, he'd managed to fill a mayonnaise jar with coins. He did it by selling tickets to a "freak show," as he called it. He'd got the idea from a circus that had rolled into town the previous winter and like them, he was advertising. I'd heard

11

that makeshift posters were plastered anywhere kids might congregate, like the baseball diamond and the swimming hole. The signs read, "Admission: 5-cents."

Thanks to him, I saw more classmates that summer than I did when school was in session. Herman's customers came like flies to a picnic. He had to be careful, though, so my parents didn't catch on.

At first, he succeeded. Dad mistook the scuffling for mice and brought home a few traps from Swanson's hardware store. That was the second night of my incarceration.

Dad was about to set a trap in the cubbyhole under the stairs when he discovered Derrick Larkin in hiding. Derrick was Herman's best friend, a timid boy who, once discovered, sang like a canary. Dad wasn't happy about what he heard and that meant Herman wasn't either.

Dawn of the third day found me cheerless as well. Even the weather had turned against me. Rain tapped at the window, and the temperature had dropped low enough to justify the use of hot water bottles. School would begin in three weeks and I was green as a cow pasture.

My eyes rolled up to the ceiling above my bed. "Lord," I whispered. "I've learned my lesson. Turn me into myself again and I won't be no more bother."

Herman rolled over in his bed when he heard me. He was wearing a stupid grin so I threw a pillow at him. That started a fight loud enough to bring Mom, Dad and Uncle Henry bursting into the room. By then, Herman and I were rolling on the floor, but Mom knew what to do. She grabbed each of her sons by an ear and began shaking us until the place fell silent.

Dad grunted his satisfaction in the peace that followed and Uncle Henry did, too. Then, satisfied that justice would be done, both men stumbled back to their beds for another hour of shut eye.

"I'm ashamed of you both, brawling like this and on a Sunday," Mom said once we were alone.

"Ollie started it."

"That's enough, Herman. I want you to go downstairs and wait for me in the kitchen."

"But I didn't do anything."

"Go!" Mom pointed toward the door and Herman obeyed, but not before sticking out his tongue at me.

Once we were alone, Mom began tidying up the place. Even after a night's sleep, she looked tired. By way of apology, I picked up the pillow I'd hurled across the room and returned it to my bed.

Mom's voice softened. "You'll be twelve soon, Oliver. Herman's only seven. You need to be an example for your little brother. He looks up to you."

"No he doesn't," I objected. "Anyway, I'm green, Mom. Nobody's gonna look up to me 'cept maybe a worm."

Mom sat on my bed and drew me to her. "Yes and we both know there's a reason why you're green, don't we?"

Looking into her wide brown eyes, so open, so searching, I felt ashamed. I'd made a mess of things over the past few days. I'd played tricks on Mr. Katafias, a gentle man with no harm in him. I'd abused a homeless cat, taken swipes at my schoolmates, and had felt sorry for no one but myself.

My face began to pucker and my eyes filled with tears. That's when Mom put her arms around me. "There's no need to cry, honey. Just think about the sort of person you want to be. If you grow up half as kind as your father, you'll be the sweetest man in the world. Brave and honest, too. That's the kind of man I want you to be."

"I'll try Mom, I will," I whispered, hugging her back.

A short while later, Mom ran a bath for me, using the crystals Mrs. Katafias had reserved for the third day. I sank into the milky water not knowing what to expect. Maybe I'd turn purple or develop fins. Whatever the outcome, I deserved my punishment.

What I noticed first were the green rivulets forming in the water.

My eyes widened in disbelief. Was it possible? Had my prayers been answered? I wasn't sure, but I began scrubbing with an evangelical zeal.

How long I stayed submerged in those waters, I do not know, but when I arose and saw my reflection in the bathroom mirror, I couldn't help but shout. "Glory hallelujah in the highest! I am saved!"

All that took place years ago, of course. But the memory of 1939 stays with me: the summer of the burlap bag. That's the year I learned not to make too much of the deviations in my fellow men -- their customs, creeds, and least of all the color of their skins.

Chapter 2 - The Night the Foreign Legion Came to Visit

Photograph: *Henry running through the sprinklers with Oliver and Herman, July 1939*

The summer of 1939 was one of the hottest on Ohio's record, a season when midnight temperatures routinely soared to 102 degrees. Those evenings, our family slept with the windows open, as did most of the community around us. The paucity of crime among the citizenry gave us no reason think that our action was unwise. Besides, my mother was a light sleeper, one who could hear a speck of dust fall in a distant room.

Why she was not more somnambulistic like Uncle Henry, was a mystery. Uncle Henry was a Rip Van Winkle, capable of sleeping through a tornado and awakening the next morning surprised to find himself sitting in a bathtub. Dad accounted for this talent by accusing his brother-in-law of being a "lay-about with his head in the clouds." Of course, he never shared his opinion with my mother, as she held her brother in a different light. She said he had an "artistic soul."

To support her opinion, she'd told Herman and me the story of Uncle Henry's youthful passion for Abigail Dimwitty, daughter of a former postmaster. Both he and Abigail were fifteen at the time, but unlike most girls her age, she had a serious turn of mind. She seldom spoke and seemed to prefer keeping her nose in books of verse, which gave Uncle Henry an idea.

Each year The Yellow Banner, the town's local newspaper,

15

sponsored a poetry contest. What better way for Uncle Henry to gain Abigail's attention and possible admiration than by entering the competition and winning the prize, which was always a volume of <u>*Leaves of Grass*</u> by Walt Whitman?

With the energy of a fly attempting to buzz its way through a pane of glass, my relative set himself to his task. Secretly, he read books, but the poems they contained failed to move him. He rather liked, "Gunga Din," but most of the verses he read talked too much about nightingales and daffodils. He wanted an idea that was fresh! And then he heard, or read, or stumbled across an extraordinary piece of information: that in all the English language there was no rhyme for the word "orange."

Like Columbus, he set off on an impossible voyage. He was determined. No! He was obsessed with the notion that he could prove the orange theory wrong and in so doing win first prize from The Yellow Banner.

To that purpose, Uncle Henry neglected his studies, which, I'm told, was nothing new to his teacher, Miss Duncan. Neglect was his habit. What did strike her as remarkable was his new found ability to sit for hours, peering out of the classroom window and never once dropping his books, or tipping his ink well, or humming.

One Saturday, while crossing Parson's grove and while chanting the word "orange" to himself over and over again, Uncle Henry failed to see a hornet's nest dangling in his path. He smacked it hard with his head -- a surprise to himself as well as to the inhabitants within -- and came home with eyes and lips swollen -- evidence he said, that hornets do not care for poetry.

Sadly, the week he spent languishing in bed recovering from his wounds brought him further injury. The Yellow Banner awarded <u>*Leaves of Grass*</u> to Sylvia Pittman for her poem, "To an Asphodel." Worse, when Uncle Henry returned to school, Abigail Dimwitty's first words to him were. "Only a fool walks into a hornet's nest!"

Unlucky in love, my mother's sibling gave up his quest for the perfect rhyme and as a result of his new acquaintanceship with Rudyard Kipling, took up the notion of joining the Foreign Legion -- a place without females and where it didn't matter whether or not you washed behind your ears. To that end, he plastered his walls with the faces of hardened men and scandalized his mother, my Grandma Westerlund, by wearing his pillowcase as a burnoose.

I suspect Uncle Henry was having another of his dreams about the Legion that summer night when Bodacious Scurvy stepped through one of our open windows. Why, after reconnoitering the place, the cat chose to make a pillow of our sleeping relative, I do not know, but the caterwaul that followed is family history. Certainly Uncle Henry, awakened by the weight upon his chest, imagined he was under attack. Certainly Bodacious Scurvy, being flung across the room, imagined the same. The skirmish that followed was marked by mass destruction and the loss of several cherished heirlooms: the blue china lamp, the hand painted washstand and the oak chair carved by Grandpa Larson for his bride-to-be.

Also destroyed was the peace of the neighborhood. Lights blinked on like fireflies and someone was heard to say, "Dollars to doughnuts, it's that crazy brother-in-law again!"

By now the entire family was huddled in Uncle Henry's room, shivering from surprise, especially Herman and I, two Methodist boys, who, that night, were privileged to hear some pretty colorful language. Bodacious, pinned under the washstand, exhibited a similar fury. His ears were flattened against his head and he hissed like a steaming kettle.

"Get that cat outta' here!" my dad bawled when he spied Bodacious. His tone was not only angry but also accusing, as if he suspected his in-law of harboring yet another mouth to feed.

17

Uncle Henry, however, was in no mood for accusations. "If ya want him outta here, do it yourself. I wouldn't touch that scurvy cat if it were wrapped in diamonds."

The two men stood at high noon, eyeing one another, a sight that always made my mother nervous. Stepping between them, she crooned to Bodacious as if he were her sole point of interest. "There, there. Poor thing. You're not a scurvy cat, are you? No, you're scared, that's all. Shall I feed you some warm milk? Hm? Shall I?"

To everyone's amazement, the cat allowed itself to be picked up and carried downstairs. Dad and Uncle Henry followed Mom with shoulders hunched like recalcitrant school boys. Herman and I were told to go to bed, but we didn't sleep even though the neighborhood went quiet again.

Until the fall, I gave little thought to Bodacious Scurvy or the Foreign Legion. That's when Nancy Gunderson arrived in town. If Abigail Dimwitty had been half as pretty as Nancy, I could see why Uncle Henry'd made a fool of himself. Nancy's curls, the color of corn tassels, bounced about her shoulders when she walked and I couldn't take my eyes off them. Most girls didn't have curls. Most girls tied their hair back or wore it bobbed. Nor did they see the world through large, violet eyes that were heavily fringed with lashes. When the new girl was assigned the seat next to me, how could I do anything but melt like spring snow?

The first week of Nancy's arrival, I could barely speak to her, let alone look into those eyes. That doesn't mean I didn't try to make contact. I did. My elbow must have crossed the boundary of our shared ink well a hundred times; but Nancy never seemed to notice. She kept to her studies and my attempt to get acquainted brought me nothing but howls from home. "Look at these ink stains, Oliver! Look at them! Do you suppose your father and I can afford to buy you a new shirt every day?"

18

By October, I was so in love with the new girl, that when she joined our church choir, I signed up, too. I tried my best to carry a tune. I truly did. But a week hadn't passed before the Pastor's wife took me aside and asked if I'd turn the music pages for the organist instead.

Banned from the choir, I had little opportunity to foster our relationship, Nancy's and mine, until November. One day, our teacher, Mrs. Wyerick, a tall, thin woman with iron gray hair and a kindly face, reminded us that as sixth graders we were responsible for the Christmas pageant. She asked for volunteers and though normally the idea of being in a play would give me hives, when Nancy's hand shot up, mine did, too. I couldn't have been more surprised. To be honest, if a line of giraffes in pink tutus had come kicking their way into the classroom I would have considered it normal compared to the sight of my hand outstretched above the others. I tried to communicate with it. "What are you doing, up there? Are you crazy?" But the hand wouldn't listen and before I could recant, I, like Nancy, was among the chosen!

At recess, Luscious Lucas, a kid who was wide as he was tall, sauntered over to the tetherball where I was waiting for my turn at play. "What's gotten into you, Larson? You ain't never wanted to be in no theatrical before. Don't suppose it's got somethin' to do with that new girl, does it? You ain't gone and got a crush on her, have ya?"

"You got rocks in your head, you know that?" was all I could think to say. Then I gave Luscious a shove, but he didn't budge.

"Erik thinks ya got a crush on her. So does Stubby."

"Erik Ladde don't know his be-hind from his ears. Neither does Stubby. I figured it was my civic duty. That's why I signed up."

"Civic duty! Ha! That's a good one! The real truth's as plain as the hairs up your nose. You got a crush on Nancy Gunderson."

"Get out of here! I don't even like her. She's forever borrowing things."

"That so? Then ya might as well tell her. She's right behind ya."

I swung round like a cat with its tail caught in a door. "I-I didn't mean it, Nancy. I-I was just..." Nancy was nowhere in sight.

Luscious grinned like he'd been handed an apple pie and danced away. "Larson loves Nancy! Larson loves Nancy." He didn't stop until he'd reached the circle where Stubby and Erik were playing marbles. They glanced in my direction. Then their laughter exploded, like BBs into the air.

At dinner that night, I confessed to the family that I'd volunteered for the play. Mom was passing the mashed potatoes at the time and nearly dropped the bowl. Dad sat with his jaw hung open but said nothing. Only Uncle Henry seemed to guess what was at the heart of my decision. He smiled then stared into distance, perhaps remembering the face of Abigail Dimwitty.

The next two weeks were bliss. Nancy and I spent most of our afternoons together in the school auditorium -- though the girls were kept to one side of the hall and the boys to the other. On stage, however, it was different. Nancy played Mary and I, as Melchior, one of the three Wise Men, stood behind her, close enough for her to hear my stomach growl. What a picture she made, dressed in white, her golden hair falling across the celluloid doll that represented the baby Jesus. She stole the scene without being given a single line. I wasn't so lucky. As it turned out, Mrs. Wyerick took it into her head that I was to introduce the tableau. My job was to shout into the audience, "Lo and behold the Son of God!"

How or why my teacher came upon this assignment I do not know. Maybe she wanted to get even with me for coming down with chickenpox and spreading it to the whole class. It couldn't be that she'd forgotten I broke into hives at the least mention of an oral report. What I do know is that when I suggested one of the other Wise Men for the job, she waved me away. "Nonsense, Oliver. You're always talking in class. You're perfect for the part!"

The afternoon of the performance, Mom baked a tuna casserole for the potluck that was to be held in the cafeteria afterwards. The play started at five, but as I was to be at school by 3:30 for make-up, Mom placed the hamper on the back porch where I would be sure to see it and take it along.

If the basket seemed too heavy, I gave it little thought. I was rehearsing my line, "Lo and behold the Son of God," repeating it over and over again, convinced that if I stopped, even for a moment, I'd forget the words entirely. Or mix them up: "Lo and behold the dung of Cod!"

By the time I reached the school yard, I'd broken into a sweat. Mrs. Wyerick was standing in the snow by the auditorium door, gazing out across the yard. She flapped her arms like a crow the moment she saw me.

"Oliver, you're late! Why, on this of all days?" Her eyes sparked with impatience the moment she saw the hamper. "Put that thing down somewhere and get into costume. There's not a moment to lose."

I found Luscious Lucas backstage. He was in charge of raising and lowering the curtain and when he saw the hamper, he offered to look after it. I doubted he could be trusted, but I had no choice. The glue on my beard was still wet when Mrs. Wyerick placed a finger to her lips to signal the actors that the play was about to begin.

The gloom of my one line hung about me like a dense cloud. I could see the misty shapes of shepherds, see the angel and the star, but it was like a dream. This state of mind might explain why, when the curtain opened on the manger scene, Joseph and Mary were there and two of the Wise Men, but Melchior was standing in the wings.

Mrs. Wyerick flapped her hands in a gesture meant to shoo me forward, but I paid no attention. I was mesmerized, rooted to the spot like someone perched at the edge of a precipice. Her whispered words, "Oliver, get on the stage," seemed hardly meant for me.

Finally, she rendered a blow that sent me sprawling on to the proscenium. Blinded by the lights, I stood like Pinocchio, waiting for someone to pull my strings. Certainly, I could no more remember my one line than I could recite all the capitals of Europe.

If I could have disappeared in a cloud of smoke like some magician's assistant, I'd have given up all my worldly goods -- my tiger's agate and even my bike. But a miracle of a different sort waited me.

At first all I heard was Mrs. Wyerick hissing from the wings: "Lo and behold the S-S-S-on of God." What followed, however, was a hissing of a different sort, one more feline and more menacing. Apparently, Bodacious Scurvy, attracted by the smell of tuna, had crept into Mom's hamper when it was on our back porch. Having devoured her casserole in its entirety, it had curled up within for a long winter's nap. Imagine its surprise at being rudely awakened by Luscious Lucas's groping hand. Imagine its outrage at being mistaken for a drumstick or a turkey leg. The cat let out a yowl and bit Luscious Lucas on the hand. The boy in turn let out a yowl of his own.

What happened next is a matter of local history. The cat bounded onto center stage, its fur stiff as cactus needles, and took refuge on Nancy Gunderson's lap. Shrieking, the girl leaped to her feet and knocked her head against the center pole, which was the base from which a multitude of tin stars were hung. The blow brought down the sky. Mary, Joseph, the two Wise Men and all the shepherds were caught in the meteoric downpour. A field of blue poplin settled like a blanket over all the players, creating the illusion that a beast, animated by the thrashing of arms, legs and elbows, occupied the stage. So distressed were its cries that the audience, most of them parents, rushed headlong on to the proscenium to rescue their offspring.

Safe to say, that day upon the stage was my first and last flirtation with the theater. Mom and Dad were sympathetic about my experience. Herman was delighted. And Uncle Henry was exuberant. He said it had been the best night's entertainment he'd seen in years.

By comparison, the rest of the Christmas holiday was uneventful. I kept a low profile. But as New Years came round and I faced the prospect of school, my thoughts turned to the Foreign Legion. One night I asked Uncle Henry if he imagined it still existed.

"You know, Oliver," he said, drawing his arms around my shoulders, "there's plenty of times when running away looks like a good idea. That's how the Foreign Legion got started. But I've learned that no man goes far in life without the opportunity to make a fool of himself. As long as men and women are around, the Legion will exist."

Chapter 3 - Proverbs

Photograph: *Oliver and Paddy O'Malley on their way to school, September, 1939*

When he wanted to, Paddy O'Malley could charm the bees away from their honey. Leastwise, that's what my mother said, "A real standout."

Had to be. He was one of two Irish kids in a sixth grade overrun with Vikings -- Larsons, Swensons, Bjorklunds, and such. I agreed with Mom. He was a born leader and I was proud to be his friend.

We didn't always get along. Sometimes, his cocksureness could be irritating. Not that I was short of that trait myself, as my little brother, Herman, was quick to point out. It was true that I'd ruined two bikes on a dare trying to vault the banks of Johnson Creek. Maybe that's why I forgave Paddy when he irked me. Except for his freckles, we were alike.

One person Paddy couldn't win over was Ray McCartney. He was the oldest kid in a family of ten, big for his twelve years and accustomed to going his own way because his dad was drunk most of the time, and his mother was worn to the bone with caring for the younger ones.

Ray even flaunted his neglect. Boasted he could stay up nights as late as he wanted. He chewed tobacco too, like a grown-up. Even so, I suspected there were limits because, on occasion, he'd arrive at school sporting a shiner about the size of his old man's fist.

That McCartney senior could flare up like a firecracker was common knowledge. That he knew more cuss words than a sailor's parrot was no secret either, especially not to my father who had been forced to haul him off to jail more than once. Not that there was any bad blood between the two men. Old McCartney knew my dad was doing his duty and that as soon as he'd turned the lock on his prisoner, he'd notify the church so that a food basket would be sent round to Mrs. McCartney. The more cynical in our parish applauded the jailings, not only as a benefit to the community but also as a blessing to the children who, during their father's absence, were bound to eat better.

In the spring of 1939, Mr. McCartney was sentenced to 30 days in the county jail for drunk and disorderly conduct. The sentence was the longest he'd been given and Mrs. McCartney, hearing it, wept into her bandana until it went from pale to dark blue. No hand, no consoling arm could quiet her quaking as she was led from the courtroom, and many a heart cracked to see her. Dad defended the judge's decision, saying it was meant to have a sobering effect upon the prisoner but he nodded, in spite of himself, when Mom observed that his notion of justice fell hardest upon the innocent.

Surprisingly, Mr. McCartney's incarceration made no impression upon his eldest. His father's absence became a license to steal. Deliveries of butter, milk and cheese soon disappeared from doorsteps. Mr. Nolan's woodpile was raided twice and eventually, it was impossible for any kid, taking the shortcut across Peninsula Park on his way to school, to avoid being hi-jacked.

Ray McCartney, being strong and well-muscled, was an expert at shinnying up a tree and swooping down again to overcome his victim. Not that any of us ever contemplated resistance. Ray stood a head taller than most of us and his fists were big as cauliflowers. No, each of us paid the tribute -- our spare change, our sack lunches -- and thought it a fair price to escape a beating. But with each passing day, our humiliation grew, to say nothing of our hunger.

One fall morning as a gang of us were walking to school, I snapped. "Damn it, Paddy! There's six of us against him. We could take Ray, if we'd a mind to. Teach him a lesson!"

A glint showed in the eyes of Erik Ladde, Stubby Norville and some of the others. They seemed to like the odds. But Luscious Lucas, a kid as wide as he was tall, snapped back. "Yeah? And what happens after that? When he hunts us down, one by one? That's what he'll do, ya know. Pick us off like we're peas on a string."

"Aw, don't be such a big baby. Ray ain't that smart. Anyway, we'll stick together, so he don't get a chance."

"Course he'll get a chance! Lessen you plan to *live* with me... in which case, Larson, I'd sooner give up my lunches!"

Stung by laughter, I stuck out my chest. "So what's *your* idea, smart guy? Go on feeding him till he gets bigger?"

"No-o-o. But, but..." Luscious let his eyes stray to the Irish kid for help. "I bet Paddy's got an idea! You do, don'tcha, Paddy?"

The boy in the green flannel shirt nodded to indicate that he did. "Ollie's right on one count. We got to do somethin' about the situation. But I figure honey draws more flies than vinegar. That's where him and me part company." He spat on the ground for emphasis.

"What?" I felt betrayed. I'd expected my best friend to support me; not put us at loggerheads. "This here's no time for one of them goofy proverbs of yours. I don't care how much honey you got, it ain't gonna keep Ray from stealing our lunches!

What we *need* is a strategy."

Paddy put a hand on my shoulder to comfort me. "Well, isn't that exactly what I am sayin'? We need a strategy."

"All right, then. You agree with me."

"As far as it goes, yes. But we don't want fisticuffs. Luscious is right about Ray. Cross him and he'll pick us off, one by one. Don't care how long it takes. That's what he'll do. We need to surprise him. Do somethin' he don't expect. My idea is for us to set up a 'rotation'. I'd go first, to test the waters, so to speak. You'd be next, Ollie. Or maybe Erik, here. Don't much matter. Main thing is *we'd* be the ones to decide who was to lose his lunch each day. And we'd make sure it was big enough so's Ray wouldn't come after the rest of us. Whatdaya think? Ya with me?"

"'Bout as far as from here as to the end of my nose!" I growled. I was standing with my thumbs locked under my suspenders, feeling supported by the laughter of Erik and some of the others. Paddy wasn't laughing, though. Nor was Luscious who kept his eyes on us as he dove into his lunch sack to draw out a snicker doodle. The crumbs tumbled like snowflakes down his blue sweater.

My friend's eyes narrowed. He stood assessing the degree of my stubbornness -- whether or not I was willing to put up a fight. I wasn't sure myself but felt pressured by the expectant ring being formed around us by our pals. A hush descended. I remember thinking that I'd give a week's allowance to see my dad come walking by on his beat. But he was nowhere in sight. Finally, Erik gave me a shove. "Go on, Larson! Tell him! Tell him his idea, stinks!"

"Stinks?" Paddy's eyebrows flew up like a pair of wings. "Is that what ya call a plan that'll save yer hides as well as yer lunches? Think ya'd prefer a fight, do ya? Ha! Ya'd run like a rabbit at the first sight of Ray McCartney. Unless, of course, you think you got a better idea. Is that it, Erik?"

The object of Paddy's disdain was taller and more athletic than his inquisitor, but when challenged was also more likely to fold. Paddy's reputation for being quick of mind as well as fists was legion. Of Erik it was said that earwax had more imagination. A match between them was no contest. Knowing this, Erik answered with a shrug and took a sudden interest in his shoes. The rest of the gang followed suit, afraid of being similarly challenged. Some stared at the ground. Others craned their necks and peered up into the bare branches of the trees.

"He didn't mean the whole idea stinks," I answered Paddy in Erik's defense. "Just this 'rotation' thing. Whatcha mean by it?"

A number of heads nodded at what I'd said, but Paddy didn't get it. He cocked his head like a dog being given a new command. "What about the word don't you understand, Ollie? Mrs. Wyerick put 'rotation' on our spelling list last week. Mean to say you can *spell* it, but ya don't know what it means? Hell! That's one for Ripley!" He snorted as he slapped his thigh, a gesture that put me in a poor frame of mind, again.

"I didn't say. I don't know what the word means. I said I don't know what it has to do with getting Ray off our backs. You're too stingy with details. Maybe you're not clear on 'em yourself. Maybe you're bluffing about this great idea of yours!"

Paddy answered me with enough sarcasm to sour a barrel of pickles. Add to that his wild gestures, his simpering tones and it was a great recipe for a fight. I kept my silence, nonetheless, because the more he talked the more I could see that his idea *was* stupid.

"Let me see if I got this right," I said, once he'd stopped for breath. "You think we should *give* Ray our lunches and not wait to be ambushed? That we should fill him so full of sandwiches and cake and cookies that he'll grow fat as a tick at a sheep convention? What? So he can't run after us? Hell, all we'd be doin' is to make life easy for him. I don't call that a plan."

For once, Paddy took no offense. He chuckled instead. "Ya never see the big picture, do ya, Ollie? This ain't just about lunches. It's about makin' friends, *and* puttin' an end to surprise. My way, no one gets shed of his chocolate cake unless'n he means to."

Luscious saw the wisdom of this logic and waggled his many chins; but I wasn't buying it.

"Listen," I argued, punching a stiff finger into Paddy's shoulder. "Nobody's been able to tame that kid. Not his pa, not Mrs. Wyerick and sure as ringworm, not you! He's a wild cub. That's what my dad says. And he ought to know. He's hauled Ray in for truancy more'n once. You want to feed McCartney something? Okay. I say we give him a knuckle sandwich!"

Cheers went up in support. Paddy, finding himself on the ropes, began shaking his finger. "Aw, come on, you guys! I ain't never steered you wrong. Who upset the geography test last week -- which you forgot to study for, Larson? And you too, Eric. Why, Amy Johnson had such a fit when I showed her that garter snake of mine, the whole class had to be let out early! And what about you, Stubby? Who fixed it so's ya could sneak into the matinee after ya lost your dime? Admit it. I've dragged you guys out of more scrapes than a shoe wadded with gum. That's why ya got to believe me when I say Ray can change. We have to be his friends. That's all! Make him feel good about hisself. Then ya know what he'll think?"

"Yeah. We're a pack chumps!"

"In your case, he might be right!" Paddy stood grinning at me. Then he crossed his eyes and wiggled his ears. I knew what he was after. He wanted me to laugh. I didn't want to but I did, in spite of myself. The others laughed, too. That's when Paddy ruffled my hair in a friendly gesture. "Hey, Ollie, you're my best friend. Remember that!"

The argument was over. Paddy had won.

At 6 a.m. the next morning, all of us gathered at the edge of town, emerging one by one out of a mist that draped itself like moss across the trees. We'd come early, counting on Ray still being asleep and were gratified to find the shack silent. Our leader carried a brown sack that was round as it was high, a sight that set Luscious Lucas's stomach to growling. Paddy reached inside for a peanut butter cookie to pacify him. That's when I noticed the words scrawled in bold, black letters across the paper.

"What's that say?" I hissed, pointing a gloved finger.

"Somethin' for Ray to think about," Paddy answered with his chest stuck out. "It says, 'Fear nothin' but doin' wrong.' Took it from a book of proverbs at the library yesterday."

"The LIBRARY!" My jaw dropped like a trap door. Astonishment registered on every face around me. "Nobody goes to the LIBRARY unless'n they have to! What's gotten into you Paddy? Horse kicked you in the head?"

31

A pair of freckled cheeks reddened. "No it didn't! And why the fuss, Ollie? There's no shame in knowin' where the library is. One of these days -- when ya learn to read -- I'll take ya inside!"

"Oh, I know where the library is, all right. Opposite the ballpark. The ballpark's where I'll be if you come looking. Not prancing 'round those moldy books like a prissy girl!" Tugging at a dandelion, I offered it to Paddy. "Here! Put this behind your ear, why don'tcha, so we can see how pretty you look!"

The shove that landed me on my backside caught me by surprise.

I sat dazed in the wet grass, feeling my spine tingle and tasting the blood that trickled from my tongue. Paddy offered no apology. "Ya had it comin'," he smirked.

Luscious didn't like to see us fight. "Y-You okay, Larson?" he said, offering me his hand.

Ignoring him, I sprang from the ground with my fists loaded. Paddy took a blow to the stomach. The whoosh of air that left him might as well have been applause. I rejoiced in it; danced a jig to its music; even let out a howl as my friend crumpled forward.

He attempted to steady himself by reaching for the sleeve of my jacket. To prevent him, I leaped to one side, but wasn't quick enough. Paddy had caught hold of me and wouldn't let go. Together we thudded to the ground, our arms and limbs so entwined that the fingers tugging at my hair might have been my own.

I clawed and kicked to gain my advantage but even as I did, the source of my anger mystified me. Paddy and I were friends. Good friends. Yet I was doing all I could to bloody him, to shame him before the guys. The pain he inflicted on me proved his intentions were the same. I fought harder, seeing no way out but violence. Even so, regret dogged me.

How long we might have struggled to do injury to ourselves I can't say; but soon after the shouting started, it stopped again. Paddy and I had barely time to see our pals skittering off in a multitude of directions. Next we heard a voice which made both of us freeze.

"What in the Sam Hill?"

Ray towered above us, raw-eyed and bare-chested, his skin an anemic shade, much like the stripe of his blue and white pajama pants, which he held in place with a string. Disheveled as he was, his black hair matted, his pant cuffs trailing in the mud, he might have seemed to a passerby no more than a neglected boy in want of an attentive parent, but to Paddy and me he was no less startling than the sudden apparition of a ghost. When he shook us hard by our collars, we knew that he was not.

"You two got nerve, comin' here at this hour, yowling like a pair of stray cats. I ought to punch ya silly; but it looks like ya done enough of that to yerselves. Thought you guys was friends. What's got into ya, anyway?" The frown on Ray McCartney's face was one of puzzlement as much as anger.

I stared at Paddy and he stared back, which is to say, neither of us knew how to answer. If Ray hadn't been part of the mix, Paddy might have pulled a face or cracked a joke and set us to laughing. But dangling in McCartney's clutches as we did, like a pair of hooked trout, humor was hard to come by.

Ray shook us like a pair of maracas. No music came out, just the sound of teeth rattling. I knew we were goners. Already I was forming a mental picture of how Paddy and I would look with shiners as blue-black as crow's wings.

That's when the inventiveness of my friend reminded me of

why I not only liked but also envied him. He started to laugh. Not a nervous titter, mind you, but a roiling, boiling guffaw, the kind that turns ears red and forces a person to snort for air. Ray dropped us as if we were hot stones.

My inclination, once free, was to head for the trees. Ray could outrun us without raising a sweat, I knew that; but if Paddy hadn't winked, I'd have bolted, all the same -- like a dog with a skunk on its trail. Instead, when he clutched his belly and crumpled forward, I did the same. When he snorted, I snorted. When he stomped one foot, so did I. We carried on that way for a couple of minutes, laughing as if our lives depended on it -- which we were sure it did.

Finally, Ray had had enough. "Cut it out! Cut it out, the pair of ya!" He raised his fists and glowered at us, which sobered me a little. But Paddy didn't blink.

"It's no use, Ray," he squeaked, gasping for breath. "Ollie can't help hisself no more'n me. Ya'd do the same, if ya could see yerself. If ya could see them blotches!"

"Blotches? What blotches?" McCartney's hands flew toward his face. "I don't see nothin'."

"On yer cheeks, yer forehead! Oops! There's another one just popped out!" Paddy danced a little jig of glee. "Pretty soon you'll look like one, big strawberry."

"Liar! I know you, ya little runt. This here's a trick. If I had blotches, I'd know it, wouldn't I? I'd feel somethin'. As it is, all I *feel* is the urge to smash your face." Ray took a swing at Paddy, who saw it coming and ducked. All that hit him was a swoosh of air. "Come on, ya little coward! Take yer medicine like a man!" The boy in pajama pants was prancing like a boxer, his eyes beady, his chin lifted.

Paddy was no fool. He kept his distance but he didn't let up on

Ray either. He gabbed on and on about those blotches. Said if Ray didn't believe him, he was to go inside and look in a mirror.

"Ya'd like that wouldn't ya? So's ya can skedaddle out of here soon as my back's turned. As if I'd be such a fool!"

Ray took a second swing at Paddy. Again, it met with air. The humiliation proved too much for him. His complexion turned the color of ketchup. Seeing it, his opponent danced with righteous glee. "I told ya so! You're nothin' but red! Red! RED! Ask Ollie if ya don't believe me. He won't lie to ya. His dad's a policeman."

Ray turned a dubious eye in my direction. His fists were still loaded, but he seemed to be considering. I didn't put much hope in it at first. Why would he trust me? In all the years we'd grown up together, I'd never given him so much as the time of day. And yet, his look was so searching and so earnest that I was embarrassed by it, overcome by a sense of unworthiness, which I could not understand.

His grunt told me he'd come to a decision. "Yer pa's a good man, Larson." He spoke quietly, almost with reverence. "Never did anyone no harm unless'n they deserved it. Don't suppose ya would dishonor him by lyin'? Naw. Ya wouldn't. So on yer father's honor, truth, now... do *you* see them blotches?"

For years, our Pastor had droned on about facing the 'horns of a moral dilemma', but not till that afternoon did I know or care about what he meant. Now I was faced with two choices, both of them bad. On the one hand, I could agree with Paddy and betray my father's teachings, or I could tell the truth and betray my friend who had lied to save us both.

This time, Paddy offered not a smile or a wink. He stood holding his breath, his eyes round as clock faces. On the ground beside him lay his forgotten lunch sack, a little worse for wear -

35

its contents smashed during our fight - but with its inscription clearly visible: "Fear nothing but doing wrong."

A knot formed in the pit of my stomach. I'd always hated Paddy's proverbs and now I knew why. My voice cracked as I answered. "No Ray. To tell the truth, I never did see any of those blotches..."

Ray threw a hard look at Paddy. "I knew you was lyin', ya little weasel! I *knew* it! Larson's twice the man you'll ever be. Ya can thank him that I don't skin ya alive! Go on now! Get outta here. And don't come back or it'll be the worse for ya!"

We sprinted toward the railroad tracks, Paddy and I, with Ray's laughter ringing like buckshot in our ears. Neither of us looked back. Not once! Not even when he called after me: "Hey Larson! Larson! You forgot your sack."

The next day, I held my tongue as Paddy gave his account of what had happened. According to him, he'd twisted Ray like a yo-yo string around little his finger. According to him, I'd nearly blown the deal. He spoke with one arm slung across my shoulder, leading everyone to suppose he was a great guy to forgive my blunders. The gang could not suppress their admiration. It shone like a campfire in their eyes.

Fall became winter and except for the season, nothing appeared changed. Paddy and I went sledding and ice fishing at the millpond, but to be honest, I could never again call up the old feelings of awe and loyalty I'd once had for my friend. He felt the same, I suspect. Least wise, we never did anything together without the gang as a buffer between us.

How long this arrangement could have survived, I don't know, but it held up for nearly a year, until Mr. O'Brien lost his farm and the family moved to Nebraska to live with Paddy's uncle. I never saw or heard from my friend again. I missed him.

Not long after, Ray McCartney left, too. He disappeared one night after his father's return from another stay in the county jail. No one went looking for the boy, though some speculated about his disappearance. Maybe he had been kidnapped, Luscious said. Or maybe his dad drove him off. The latter seemed likely. Anyway, his memory faded with the ebb and flow of everyday life. I had no occasion to think of him until twenty years later when his name blazed across the headlines of every newspaper in Ohio. Ray McCartney was the first prisoner in our state to be put to death in the electric chair.

Chapter 4 - Brief History of the Marabar Diner

Photograph: *Herman, Oliver and John seated at the counter of the Marabar Diner, September, 1939*

One afternoon in late spring, I went to look for my dad at the Marabar Diner to get permission to take a field trip with my sixth grade class. Looking around the place, which was long and narrow, I was reminded that someone had said it'd been a caboose in its earlier days. There was little evidence of that now. The outside had been covered with shingles and painted green. Anyway, its history didn't interest me as much as its name, 'Marabar'. The word sounded exotic and full of mystery -- not like 'Ingrid's Bake Shoppe' or 'Swanson's Hardware & Supplies', names which graced our main street.

When I found my dad, I gave him the permission slip from Mrs. Wyerick, my teacher, and waited for him to sign it, fingering the plastic covered menu lying on the table as I did. The name of the diner was printed along the top in bold, black letters. That reminded me to ask why the place was made to sound foreign. Dad didn't answer at first. He was too busy glaring at the permission slip stretched between his hands.

"Don't you bring back any animal, Oliver," he said with a sour expression. "You understand that. I don't care how cute and cuddly it is."

"No sir." I nodded, as earnestly as I knew how.

Dad scratched his head. "Why does Mrs. Wyerick want to take you to the Humane Society anyway? What are you supposed to learn there?"

"Dunno." I shrugged. "Maybe it has to do with Mr. Wyerick being the head of it."

"Maybe." Dad signed the note and shoved it back at me. "No pets, Oliver! Got it?"

"Yes sir."

He didn't have to warn me about pets. I'd heard his lecture against bringing home strays a million times. My little brother, Herman, could recite the words in his sleep. Why our father refused to allow animals at home was a question neither of us could answer.

"I'll bet he got bitten when he was a kid," my brother offered one night. He was lying in his bed with his hands clasped behind his neck as he stared up at the ceiling.

I shook my head and reminded him that Dad had broken up a bank robbery a while back. "He ain't afraid of no dogs."

"Well, what do you think the reason is?" Herman asked, turning to look at me.

If I'd been a better person, I might have ignored the temptation being offered. But Herman was eight, four years younger than I, so how could I resist making him the butt of one of my beautiful jokes? "I reckon it has something to do with a great tragedy in his life. Yep. That's it. A great tragedy."

"Tragedy!" Herman squeaked like a hinge and sat up.

"Dad's lived in this town his whole life. Nothing tragic ever happened here. Nothing EVER happens here. Rip Van Winkle coulda slept a thousand years in this town and when he woke up things would be the same."

"That shows you how much you know," I snuffled. "I guess you never heard about the tragedy up at Pilgrim's Cave."

"What tragedy?" Herman tossed me a vinegary expression that was clear to see in the moonlight. He knew I couldn't be trusted. He was still smarting from a lie I'd told him about Monopoly money being real. Miss Ingrid at the Bake Shoppe had sent him packing when he'd tried to buy a doughnut with one of its $100 bills.

"A real tragedy, about twenty-five years back when Dad was a boy." I tried to sound innocent of any past wrongs. "I guess you've forgotten."

If there was one sure thing about my little brother, it was his gall. He wasn't going to admit he'd never heard of any tragedy happening at Pilgrim's Cave.

"Oh, that tragedy," he echoed, settling down beneath his covers again. "Sure, everyone knows about that. Something about a cat, wasn't it?"

"You don't remember anything about the tragedy," I snorted. "You're pretending. The story's got nothing to do with cats."

"Oh yeah. I remember now. It's about a crime. A horrible massacre. Or was it about ghosts? I'm not sure."

I snorted again and told him he was making an idiot of himself. "It's about bats. Giant, man-eating bats that used to live up at Pilgrim's Cave."

When he heard that, Herman snorted back. "There ain't no man-eating bats up at Pilgrim's Cave. I've caught plenty of those critters. They're little things, not much bigger than my

41

thumb."

"That's all you know," I insisted. "Back when Dad was a kid, they were bigger than eagles and strong enough to carry off a boy or a dog in the blinking of an eye."

"That's a fib and you know it." Herman threw me a righteous look, but from the way his eyebrows lifted, I knew I had him hooked.

"I tell you they were strong. And that's why I'm guessing Dad doesn't want any animals around the house. He doesn't want to take any chances in case those bats come back. Not after what happened to Yuban."

"Yuban. Who's he? What happened to him?"

"I thought you said you knew all about the tragedy."

"Yeah, but I forget the details. Tell me again."

"Crimenetly, you got the brain of a sieve. Okay, I'll tell ya, but you better listen up good. One day your life may depend on it."

"I'm listening."

"Well, you remember the name of Dad's best friend when he was growing up, don'tcha?"

"Neils. Neils something..."

"That's right. And he had that big Airedale. A mean critter. A 125 pounds and as happy to bite off a person's hand as get a pat on the head."

"I remember."

"Then you remember the story Dad told about the night that dog went missing."

"'Course I do. It was a dark and stormy night."

"It was no such thing. It was August and it was hot and there was a big old harvest moon."

"Oh right. I forget the details."

"Tsk, tsk. You're beginning to sound like old Mr. Katafias. 'Where's my glasses? Where'd I leave the evening paper?'"

"Never mind," Herman bristled. "Get on with the story."

"But you know how it ends? You couldn't have forgotten something so horrible?"

"I haven't forgotten. Maybe I want to make certain you remember it right."

"A test is it?"

"Yeah. A test."

I leaned forward in my bed, close enough for Herman to hear me with my voice barely above a whisper. "All right then. But don't blame me if the details give you nightmares."

Herman shook his head. "They won't. Don't you worry about that."

"Okay then. It was a hot August night when Neils stole from his bed to search for Yuban."

"Yuban? Was that the dog's name?"

"You sure do forget a lot. Yeah, that was its name."

"That's a stupid name."

"Not if you remember how the story ends. You do, don'tcha?"

"I said I did, didn't I? Did Dad go with Neils?"

"No. Neils went alone. It was late, remember? Anyway, he headed for Pilgrim's Cave, certain those bats had kidnapped his Airedale and had tied him up so they could eat him later."

"Tied him up? Bats can't do that no matter how big they are!"

I paused, realizing that Herman's point was well taken.

"What I meant to say was that they trussed him up in their webs so he couldn't escape."

"Webs? Bats don't spin webs, do they?"

"I told you, these were special bats. They could spin webs thicker than ropes. Dad said so, remember?"

Herman sat for a moment with he eyes rolled back in his head as if he were searching for a lost memory.

"Y-Yeah. I-I think so. But if they could spin webs, how come Neils wasn't afraid those bats would catch him and truss him up too?"

"I suspect the thought occurred to him. That's why he waited until midnight when the bats were out looking for prey and it was so dark a person couldn't see his hand before his face."

"I thought you said there was a harvest moon."

"Not inside the cave, ya fool!"

"Oh. Okay then. Go on."

"So, Neils is at the mouth of the cave and he can hear a stirring inside, so deep that the sound echoes in waves like a moan."

"Ghosts ya mean?"

"Yeah, just like that. For sure, it wasn't human."

"Is it the dog, ya think?"

"Could be. Anyway, Neils intends to find out. He hunkers down and heads for that moan with a slow and steady step."

"What if it ain't the dog? What if it's his ghost?" Herman shuddered.

By now I'd left my bed and was standing close enough to see my kid brother's eyes. They were gleaming in the moonlight like two half dollars. "Will you shut up?" I told him. "I'm getting to the good part now."

Herman fell silent and watched as my hands - like they'd been tied to balloons -- rose to shoulder height. I shuffled toward him like a sleep walker and started to moan. "Yuban... Yuban... Yuban..."

Herman shuddered again and leaned away. "I-Is that what Neils said? Are you acting his part?"

His eyes had grown to the size of frying pans. Seeing him like that, and with his hair stuck out at right angles, I couldn't contain myself. I doubled up with laughter. "Yuban!" I cried. "Yuban had, Herman! There weren't no tragedy at Pilgrim's Cave. And you're a fool for pretending."

Herman's pillow flew past my head as I took a bow.

While my father's aversion to pets remained a mystery, I was determined to satisfy my curiosity about the diner's name. The strangeness of it kept hiccupping in my brain.

"Marabar's the name of some cave in a novel," Dad conceded when it was clear I would not disappear.

"A novel? Which one?"

"*A Passage to India*, I think."

"India! That figures. It didn't sound like a Scandinavian name."

"No. It's about a cave where some mysterious forces are at work."

I edged forward and put my face next to Dad's, as if something delicious was about to be revealed. Maybe some Indian pirates had once sailed up the Mississippi and buried treasure right there, under the floor of the Marabar diner. "What mysterious forces?" I whispered. "Where?"

"I don't know, Oliver." Dad turned his attention to his coffee. "I never read the book. Oscar'll have to tell you. He's the one who named the place. It used to be called 'Joe's'."

Oscar, the proprietor stood a few stools down the counter, pouring coffee for a stranger who'd asked how many miles it was to Springfield. Apparently he'd been listening with half an ear.

"Doesn't this place seem like a cave, Ollie? Look around."

I did as he suggested and after a brief reconnoitering, I had to admit there was a decided resemblance. The walls of the diner were dingy and the red checkered curtains had faded into pink - so had the counter top and the linoleum flooring. On the surface, the place was cheerless even on the sunniest day. But people made the Marabar interesting: the farmers and especially the truck drivers who came in with their sleeves rolled up to their elbows, men who drank endless cups of coffee and talked about towns named Catawaba, Shawnee and Moxabala.

"Maybe it does look like a cave, sir. But why name the diner after some place in India? Why not call it 'Pilgrim's Cave'?"

Despite the fiction I'd fed to Herman, Pilgrim's cave had an interesting history in its own right. That bat cave in the hills above the town was named after an eccentric called Francis Pilgrim. He'd stumbled on to it about a hundred years earlier and became obsessed with the idea of turning the place into a dance hall. On the surface, it was a pretty good idea -- being it was far enough from town to avoid the attention of stiff-necked citizens who were opposed to a bit of fun and close enough to attract those who weren't.

Apparently, Mr. Pilgrim spent a wad of money driving out the bats and cleaning up the place, as bats are not particular about their habits. Then he bought some tables and chairs and kerosene lamps and when he stumbled upon three farm boys who said they could make music, he announced the date of the opening. A few posters went up in discreet places around town, but mostly the news was spread by word of mouth and on the first Saturday in July, Mr. Pilgrim got himself ready to make a fortune.

A few customers arrived at 6 p.m., milling around with their arms looking long at their sides until the Hi-Ho Foot Stompers arrived -- a little late because of some trouble with a plough. When the fiddling began the music spilled out of the cave and floated toward the town so that more people came, and by 8 p.m. the place was packed with customers enjoying a surfeit of music and moonshine.

As the story goes, Mr. Pilgrim stood behind his table and smiled as cash poured into his shoe box. His one regret, he told a patron, was that Mrs. Pilgrim wasn't around to witness his success. She'd scoffed at his idea. Said a cave wasn't a fit place to hold a dance. And what about those bats?

The bats, Mr. Pilgrim is said to have informed her, hadn't been invited. Still, he confessed, he wouldn't hold his wife's laced-up opinions against her. He'd earned enough money that night to buy her a hat -- one with crow feathers stuck into the brim. She'd understand.

By dawn, with the dancers turning tired circles in the dust, Mr. Pilgrim began to count his money. Absorbed as he was, he failed to hear the drone of a thousand bat wings flapping in the direction of their ancestral home.

No one had time to escape before the cave was filled with their numbers. They formed a cloud so dense that they seemed not a horde but a single, demonic beast. To defend themselves against this assault, the dancers beat their arms about their heads in concert with the creature's movements, as did the Hi-Ho Foot Stompers. This dance or pagan ritual, as it might have seemed to a passer-by, went on for some time and with disastrous effect. Furniture was toppled and flung into far off spaces. Lanterns sputtered in the dirt and cries, barely human, could be heard all the way to the valley floor.

Needless to say, the opening night of Mr. Pilgrim's dance hall was also its last. After paying for the damage done to his patrons, there was barely enough money to buy Mrs. Pilgrim a hat, which she insisted was her due for being right about the bats. She chose an expensive one, without crow feathers and piled high with tulle.

After thinking about the cave and its history, I decided that 'Pilgrim's' wouldn't be a good name for the diner. But, as to why it was called Marabar, I never did get an answer. An idea came to me years later. Everyone knew the proprietor was a man of few words, but I grew to know him as a man who had ways of making a statement. The name of his diner had to be foreign. Oscar Leobwitz was the only Jew in town.

Chapter 5 - Saying Goodbye

Photograph: *John in front of the Halvorson home, walking his beat on the far side of town, September, 1939*

Joey Halvorson, who was five, didn't know his mother was dying from a weak heart but his father did and it made Mr. Halvorson gruff with him and his older brother, Craig. My mom said the sight of the boys, their eyes often moist with tears, made her heart break and that someone should talk to the father about giving more comfort to his sons. Dad knew the suggestion was meant for him. Being a town constable, people often thought he could restore order even in the human heart. Dad knew better.

"The Depression's barely over, and now Carl's about to lose his wife. If it was happening to me, I doubt I'd manage any better. Give him some time, Elsie. He loves his kids. He'll do what's right." Mom nodded, knowing that the cabinetmaker was a decent man.

But, on the other side of town where the Halvorsons lived, word was that Claire Halvorson worried about her husband's state-of-mind. He needed to accept what was happening. Unless he did, who was going to fend for the boys, particularly in domestic matters? Joey and Craig had been taught to pick up after themselves, but Carl showed no similar aptitude. And when faced with the kitchen stove, though he could wield any number of wood crafting tools, he was helpless as a newborn.

The nearest female relative lived in Nebraska with a husband

and three boys of her own, so Mrs. Halvorson was forced to consider the choices left to secure her family's domesticity. Joey was too young for responsibility and Carl seemed paralyzed. Craig was old enough, being twelve, but to place a boy in charge of the household seemed a hard fate. Nonetheless, on a fine spring morning, Mrs. Halvorson took her oldest son aside and explained that this baseball season, his time would be spent in the kitchen.

Craig knew how to sweep and clean already and he had helped with the dishes since he was eight; but he showed little aptitude for cooking, especially when he could hear the crack of a baseball bat outside his window. His mother persisted. She had no choice. With patience and repetition, she taught him the basics: how to scramble an egg, assemble a stew, and mix a mayonnaise dressing. Making a roast came easy, too, but baking was a skill that eluded him.

The luxuries, she knew, pies, cakes and cookies, could be purchased from Miss Ingrid's Bake Shoppe. Such stuff wasn't a necessity. Bread was. Unless someone in the family mastered the art, there'd be none on the table. Carl's work wasn't steady enough to afford store bought bread on a daily basis.

Mrs. Halvorson renewed her efforts with Craig, pulling down her prized recipe books to help her explain terms like scaling, kneading, and creaming, words which to most boys were a mystery. Craig listened to his mother's lectures with a glazed expression. He took no pride in this new knowledge -- even felt ashamed. The weight of his duty made his shoulders droop and his feet dragged whenever he approached the kitchen.

Mrs. Halvorson grew desperate. In her efforts to impress her son, she showed him pictures of world famous chefs, men who were rich and famous. Craig shrugged. "Maybe some ladies admired these guys," he said. "But the whole world knows Babe Ruth."

One afternoon when she was so weary there were tears in her eyes, Mrs. Halvorson sat beside her son at the kitchen table. With her hands stretched out in front of her, she began to cross and uncross her fingers as she searched for the words to reach him. Finally, she spoke from the heart.

"I need you to try harder, Craig. Because one day... well, things will be up to you. Your father, Joey, they can't... You understand what I'm saying, don't you? I couldn't rest if the family had to go without. I couldn't..."

They were close enough for their elbows to touch; close enough for Craig to see the pallor of his mother's skin, the hollows around her blue eyes. A lump formed in his throat. He nodded to indicate that he would try. Then Mrs. Halvorson cried and Craig cried with her.

Despite his promise, Craig's failures in the kitchen mounted. The more his mother prodded, the more disastrous the outcome. Yeast breads were ruled out. Craig's fingers couldn't sense the desired texture. The dough was either too hard or too sticky -- never pliant.

Mrs. Halvorson moved on to quick breads: muffins, corn bread, and soda biscuits. These recipes required nothing more than mixing. She delivered her instructions slowly, as though she had tar in her mouth. Craig needed to understand because she hadn't much time.

To Joey, the sight of his brother standing beside his mom, floured from his elbows to his nose, was a source of amusement. He laughed and pointed and made the rude noises younger brothers did. Sometimes he wanted to help, which was more exasperating than the teasing. Craig held his temper because he knew Joey didn't understand. Sometimes he threatened to douse his little brother with salt, which sent the child scurrying. But Joey always came back. Whatever Craig was up to in that kitchen looked like a marvelous game.

Not long after the lessons had begun, Mrs. Halvorson died. During the period of mourning there wasn't much activity in the kitchen. The neighbors saw to it that there was no need. They brought soups and stews and platters of meats intended to keep the survivors nourished. These offerings grew in quantity until large portions had to be thrown away. Bodacious Scurvy, the town's renowned alley cat, spent a good deal of time at the Halvorson's during those days. The family encouraged him to do so as he was the only lodger with an appetite.

A week passed, then two, and Mrs. Halvorson's death, which began as a grief for her family, now became a torment. Her absence haunted them like a presence -- a fog that shrouded their hearts and forced them to drift about the house as if they, too, had become unearthly spirits. Beds went unmade. Meals were forgotten. A little soap and water seemed all that was required, habits Mrs. Halvorson had insisted upon and out of love for her they honored. But beyond the morning and evening ablutions, time had no meaning.

Life at the Halvorson's might have gone on unraveling that way but for Joey. Too small to care for himself, he made demands. A button needed sewing or he was hungry; and so, with difficulty, the ebb and flow of daily routine insinuated itself into the life of the family. Mr. Halvorson returned to his workshop; Craig returned to the kitchen.

Glancing about him, Craig saw his neglect of his mother's domain and felt ashamed. He vowed to do better and aligned the dirty plates in neat stacks upon the green and white tiled counter. The order he was imposing gave him a sense of purpose and almost cheerfully, he sank his arms into the soapy water that filled the sink. By late afternoon, he had finished his work and stood admiring the shine he'd put on the kitchen floor. That's when Joey bounded in to ask about supper.

Supper? Craig peered at the clock above the ice box and

muttered something about where the time had gone. Joey said he knew nothing about the time except that he was hungry. Craig handed his little brother an apple, then reached for one of his mother's treasured cookbooks.

Fannie Farmer fell into his hands. The name, Fannie, had always made Craig smirk, but this time there was something magical about the way the pages fell open to the section on breads. The words, "A simple recipe for soda biscuits" flew up at him. The boy peered around the room, half expecting to see his mother smiling; but he was alone. Still, he took the incident as a sign and placed himself in the hands of Fannie Farmer, a woman he did not know and whom he imagined had a beaked nose and wore thick glasses. He pre-heated the oven, as instructed, assembled the ingredients, of which there few, and wiped his hands on his trousers in nervous anticipation.

Except for cutting in the lard, the preparation was fluid, almost as if his mother's hands were guiding his. True, he lost track of his measurements once or twice but the dough seemed to be forgiving. It filled the bowl with a white, sticky substance that was a pleasure to see.

Craig set the bowl aside and turned to the stew. Everything was going well and for a moment he forgot the tragedy that had brought him to these tasks. He basked instead in the joy of his accomplishment. Cooking was like baseball. It was a skill where timing, coordination and a sharp eye meant the difference between success and failure. Craig had never understood why his mother took such pleasure from her labors. He understood now. He was in her head, and although she was gone, he felt closer to her at that moment than during the time of his whooping cough when she had rocked him in her lap all night.

At six o'clock the family sat down to dinner, the first time they had gathered at the kitchen table since the funeral. Mrs.

Halvorson's chair was empty and Mr. Halvorson refused to look at it. No one made any reference to her absence. Joey, who'd been playing in the mud out back, was sent to wash up twice before passing inspection. His whining brought an air of normalcy to the setting.

In silence, Craig ladled out the stew. He set the steaming bowls before his father and brother, then stepped back to review his work, the way an artist pauses before his canvas. What he saw pleased him. He had surpassed his mother's rudimentary requirements and created a feast for the eye as well as for the belly. What more could be asked of him? "Nothing," pride might have answered; but pride was not seated at the table. His father was and he wanted to know if there was any bread.

The off-handedness of the question spoke volumes to Craig about his father's ignorance of culinary matters. How bread came to be provided; what efforts were expended to create it and the pitfalls that might occur in its making, seemed to be taken for granted. Bread, his father must have imagined, was the consequence of magic.

Craig hid his disappointment. "Sure, there's bread," he said, turning to the stove. "Biscuits. I made 'em this afternoon."

Joey's eyes followed his brother's. "Biscuits! Where'd you learn to do that? Are they any good?"

Craig didn't answer. His mouth had gone dry and his eyes were fixed upon the oven door. Had he remembered to add salt? Soda? Was there enough lard in the mixture? A thousand doubts assailed him and made him hesitate. Cooking, he decided, was nothing like baseball. Cooking was harder.

His father offered words of encouragement. "Smells good, son. Think they're about ready?"

Craig peered into the oven, saw the silhouettes of the plump biscuits and uttered a sigh. "Thank you Fannie Farmer. Thank you!" He could not have been more grateful if Babe Ruth had offered to autograph his baseball bat. The same euphoria swept over him. Unfortunately, it was brief.

"What are those things?" Joey snickered as the pan hit the table. His father looked surprised as well. Anyone could see the biscuits were as high and firm as pillows, but they were... green.

The youngest Halvorson poked at one to see if it would jump. When it didn't, the father admonished the boy, saying that looks weren't everything. As he reached for one of the pillows and bit into it, the mouths of both his boys dropped open.

"Is it okay, Dad? Did I get it right?"

Mr. Halvorson drained his coffee cup and poured out a second before answering.

"Ya did fine, son. Just fine." The words were reassuring, but the voice faltered so that it cast some doubt upon their truth. Suspicious, the five-year-old folded his arms in front of him when the tray was shoved in his direction.

"They look diseased!" Joey said, squinting at them.

Mr. Halvorson shook his head. "Your brother worked hard to make us this supper. The least you could do is show some appreciation."

The youngest son knew his father was right, but he didn't want to be a guinea pig. He wanted his mama to make him biscuits the way she used to -- round, white morsels that with butter and a little honey tasted like pastry. He wanted the smell of cake wafting from the oven and to see jars of peaches lined up in the cupboard. But most of all, he wanted his mama.

Craig saw his brother hesitate and lost patience. "Oh, come

now! These biscuits aren't that bad!" To make his point, he bit into one, letting the crumbs cascade down his chin. The texture was light, like those of Mrs. Halvorson's. And as for the salt, he'd remembered that, too, and the soda. Maybe he'd remembered too much soda. That would account for the biscuit's green overcast and for the briny taste that assaulted Craig's tongue. Suddenly, his mouth went prickly and started to pucker. Swallowing a porcupine would be easier, he thought.

Craig sprang to the sink intending to wash away the stinging sensation but in his hurry, he twisted the tap too hard. The water gushed forth in an uncontrolled stream. It left him soaked and standing in a puddle two inches deep. The stream was still gushing as he caught sight his reflection in the porcelain basin. The frown he saw there was enough to startle him. He realized that he had been furious with his mother. She shouldn't have left them. They needed her. It wasn't fair.

Knowing his thoughts were foolish, Craig struck his fist against the counter in anger. He had to be a man now, not a boy. He owed that much to his mother.

Craig turned to face the remains of his family, half expecting to see disappointment reflected in their eyes. He couldn't have been more wrong. What he saw was a pair of grinning faces.

His dad spoke with a twinkle in his eye, the first seen in many weeks. "Did ya drink the tap dry, son? I was afraid I might have to wade in to save you from drowning."

"Yeah," Joey piped up. "Leave some for us, will ya?"

Craig's smile was hesitant. "Don't worry. There's plenty of water left if anyone wants another biscuit."

"NO thank you!" The youngest Halvorson submitted his protest by tossing one of the green abominations into the pool at Craig's feet. Together, they watched as it dissolved like a salted slug. Mr. Halvorson threw in a second and Craig a third. Then the room exploded into laughter.

Such gaiety might have surprised a passerby, knowing that death had been a recent visitor to that house. But under the lamp that glowed above the kitchen not only was the dark being held at bay but healing was beginning. Mr. Halvorson, Joey, Craig were glad at least in this: they had each other.

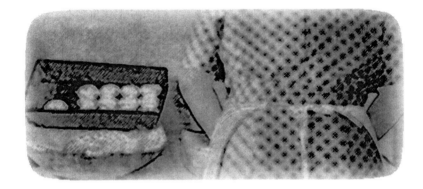

Chapter 6 - Of Ghosts, Goblins, and Little Green Men

Photograph: *Herman and Oliver get Ready to put on their ghost costumes, October 1939*

After the episode of the burlap bag where I turned green, I should have learned my lesson about the dangers of playing pranks. but, seeing how my little brother turned a profit from my misfortune, I decided that he was owed. I'd been playing with the kernel of an idea even before the mishap, the previous Halloween, 1938, when Herman and I planned to don a pair of bed sheets and masquerade as ghosts. We were lying on the living room floor at the time, arguing over who was bound to collect the most candy, while Mom, Dad and Uncle Henry sat around the Philco radio, listening to Edgar Bergen and his dummy, Charlie McCarthy on the *Chase and Sanborn Hour*.

"Will you two keep quiet? We can't hear a thing with the pair of you making a ruckus."

As Dad spoke, a commercial for "Old Spice Aftershave" came on and not being one who could sit still, he got up from his chair and spun the radio dial to see what else might be going on. That's when we heard an urgent voice come over the airwaves with an announcement.

"Ladies and gentlemen, we interrupt a program of dance music to bring you a special message from the International Radio News. At twenty minutes before eight, Central time, Professor Farrell of the Mount Jennings Observatory, Chicago, Illinois, reports observing several explosions of incandescent gas occurring at regular intervals on the planet Mars. The spectroscope indicates the gas to be hydrogen and moving toward the earth at enormous velocity."

"What the?" Dad scratched his head as the announcement ended and dance music poured through the speaker again as if nothing out of the ordinary had occurred. Confused, he spun the dial a second time, hoping to hear what the other stations were saying about the mysterious gas coming from Mars. All of us were disappointed when we heard nothing but regular programming. By the time the *Chase and Sanborn Hour* turned up, Charlie McCarthy was poking fun at Mr. Bergin, as usual.

We sat listening to the dummy's jokes with an air of incredulity, not knowing what to think about the hydrogen gas headed in our direction. Herman's only hope was that school would be closed the next day.

That's as far as his speculation got because Dad couldn't sit still. He'd swung the dial back to where we'd heard the announcement from the observatory only to learn that the situation had gotten worse.

"Ladies and gentlemen, this is the most terrifying thing I have ever witnessed." The voice coming over the airwaves seemed to be gasping for breath as it described what appeared to be a space craft with its hatch opening. "I can see peering out of that black hole two luminous disks... are they eyes... It might be a face..."

When Dad heard that, he let go of the radio dial as if it were a hot poker. "What in tarnations?" He continued to stare at the box as we learned that the counties of Mercer and Maddox in New Jersey had been put under martial law.

By now, Mom had risen to her feet to stand beside her husband.

"What is it, John? What's happening? Why are all those people screaming?"

"I don't know, Elsie. Listen a minute."

Uncle Henry, Herman and I jumped to our feet too, all of us staring at the radio as if we were at a picture show. What followed were a number of bulletins hastily read one after another. Washington DC was sending the Red Cross to Grover's Mills, the area where the broadcast was coming from. The farm in question had been cordoned off and the New Jersey state militia was taking over the airwaves in the national interest.

Then a man who introduced himself as Captain Linton started to speak, "Hello... hello. Am I on?"

Before he could say anything useful, the announcer cut in again, breathless and terrified as well. "Ladies and gentleman, as incredible as it may seem, both the observation of science and the evidence of our eyes leads to the incredible assumption that these strange beings who have landed in the Jersey farmland tonight are the vanguard of an invading army from the planet Mars."

Everyone in our living room took a step backwards, as if ordered to do so. ''John, what does this mean? What should we do?" Mom was clinging to Dad's arm as if it were a rope meant to keep her from falling off the edge of a cliff. Dad didn't answer at first. He was listening to a new voice coming out of the bowels of the Philco, a voice that identified itself as the Secretary of the Interior. It confirmed that an invasion was underway though, at the moment, it was confined to the rural area of New Jersey.

"J-John? What do we do?"

"I've got to call the station, Elsie. I'll see what they know.

Everyone sit down. We're a long way from the East Coast, so don't panic." Dad headed for the telephone while the rest of us perched on the arm of a chair or the couch ready to run into the night at the first encouragement. Uncle Henry sat drumming his knees with his fingers while Mom glanced about the room as if taking an inventory of what to pack .Herman and I sat stupefied but, being too young to appreciate the danger, we were exhilarated too. Both of us had read of Martian invasions in our comic books and had talked about what we'd do if it ever happened.

Herman's idea was to climb a tree where he was sure the creatures from outer space wouldn't see him. But when I asked what he'd do when he had to pee, he scratched his head.

"I'll pee up there," he said finally. "Those aliens won't know any better. If it lands on 'em they'll think it's rain."

"Aw, that's a stupid idea," I scoffed. ''You can't pee up a tree. You'll get yourself wet."

"Then what're you gonna do?" Herman's jaw was squared.

"Me? I'm going to the library. No creature in its right mind would look there."

Herman wrinkled his nose as he rolled the idea over in his mind. "You're right," he nodded, "They'd be too smart already. I'm comin' with you. They got toilets at the library."

Since Herman and I had a plan, we weren't worried about an invasion. Naturally, we'd invite Mom and Dad and Uncle Henry to come with us, certain they'd be bound to see the wisdom of our thinking.

While my brother and I sat confident in our future, the chatter from the radio grew louder and more chaotic. We couldn't hear what Dad was saying on the telephone but I felt lucky that we had one. Not everyone did.

Anyway, the sounds emanating from the radio were those of a battlefield. The soldiers were measuring their target:

"One hundred and forty yards to the right, sir."

"Shift range...thirty-one meters."

The gun fired and we could hear the men coughing and choking from the smoke afterwards.

Mom sat by the Philco, wringing her hands and staring into the hallway where the telephone was located. Finally, Dad came back, his face a mottled field of grey and crimson, grey about the lips and eyes, crimson on the cheeks and forehead. Mom leapt to her feet as did Uncle Henry.

"What did they say at the station?"

"I couldn't get through, Elsie. The line's busy. Everyone with a telephone must be calling to find out what's going on. I better get down there. The rest of you stay put. It's no more'n a ten minute walk. I'll come running if there's any news." Dad cast a beady eye in Herman's and my direction as he put on his coat. "Stay inside, you hear?"

A minute later he was gone and the rest of us hovered around the broadcast to learn how our soldiers were doing. It didn't sound good. Uncle Henry started running his hands through his hair and saying he ought to do something. Mom objected.

"You heard John. We're to stay put. Don't go getting any crazy ideas. I don't need 'crazy' right now!" Mom stopped and bit her lip, sorry for the sharp way she'd spoken. Her voice was softer when she added, "I know you're going to be sensible, Henry. The boys and I need you. Besides, we don't know anything yet."

Despite the apology in his sister's tone, Uncle Henry looked taken aback. "You've no call for alarm, Elsie. You know I'm not crazy. I've always done right by the family, haven't I?"

With the tension between Mom and our uncle putting a strain on all of us, the drama unfolding over the air waves was forgotten. Mom had never snapped at her brother before, never hinted that he had a weakness. The trembling of her lips revealed that she was sorry, but she couldn't deny what she'd said and anyone could see that Uncle Henry was crushed by it.

"I didn't mean..." Mom headed toward her brother to console him, but she hadn't gone far when someone started pounding at our front door. "Elsie, are you home? Is John there?" The voice of Mrs. Katafias rose above her knocking. She was still talking through the door as Mom backed into the hall, her eyes fixed on her brother with a look of contrition.

"Yes, yes, I'm here. I'm coming," she said as she hurried to answer her neighbor's call.

Herman and I followed in time to see Mr. and Mrs. Katafias burst into the hall without waiting for an invitation. "Have you been listening to the radio, Elsie?" said the older woman. "Is it true about the invasion? Where's John? Has he gone to the station? They say the Martians have landed." Mrs. Katafias' hand flew to her cheek as she stared at her husband. "Lord have mercy upon us. What shall we do?"

The old man said nothing, as was his habit, but the worry in his eyes spoke for itself. Mom ushered the old couple into the living room as she tried to comfort them. She'd barely settled them into a pair of overstuffed chairs when there was a second knock at the door. This time it was the Hjalmers with their daughter, Ione, and her boyfriend, Kermit.

"W-We're sorry to bother you, Elsie," Mrs. Hjalmer stammered, "but Kermit's been listening to the radio and he says... I know this is going to sound ridiculous..."

Kermit Dietrick broke in, preferring to speak for himself. "It's a Martian invasion. You can hear it on the radio if you tune in."

"We are listening," Mom said as she guided the Hjalmers and Kermit toward the parlor. She had taken about three steps when there was a third knock at the door. This time, several of our neighbors stood on the porch looking anxious. Among them was old Mr. Dimwitty who was partially deaf. He said he'd heard that the Maritime had landed and he wanted my Dad to explain why the navy was invading a landlocked state. "If they want somewhere to go, they should ship over to Europe and fight that nutcase, Adolf Hitler," he bellowed.

Mom didn't try to clarify the situation but waved the visitors in as if she were a traffic cop. By now the living room was getting crowded. With everyone talking at once, people stopped listening to the broadcast. It didn't seem to matter, any more. The invasion was taken as fact. What worried people was how to accommodate these new arrivals. Did they live in houses? Drink milk?

"What if they're Catholics?" Mrs. Carlson, our church elder shuddered.

Arthur Dimwitty insisted upon his solution.

"Put uniforms on 'em. Sign 'em up for the Maritime and ship 'em over to Europe." He was brandishing a bayonet he'd brought to ward off the invaders.

Everyone stared at Mr. Dimwitty, which made him think they approved of his idea, so he repeated it a second time.

"Maybe I should make some coffee," Mom said in the lull that followed. She headed for the kitchen with me in tow and was wondering if she had enough cookies to go around when we heard another rap on the door insistent like machine gun fire.

"Get that for me, Oliver. Whoever it is bring them in and tell them to sit down if they can find a place."

I did as Mom asked, but when I saw who was standing on the threshold, I'd have preferred to see a Martian. Mrs. Duncan was the last person I'd want to get comfortable in our living room. She'd been my second grade teacher a few years back and we never took to one another. She complained that I was lazy but I felt Mrs. Duncan was the problem. She was old and pigeon-chested, which I didn't mind, or the fact that she favored the girls over the boys in her class. What I did object to was her habit of stuffing hankies up her sleeve. They were forever falling on the floor which meant that some poor kid had to retrieve them. Usually, that was me because I was seated by her desk in the front row where she could keep an eye on me.

And hankies weren't my only problem. I was allergic to her perfume, lavender, which she wore in such quantities that whenever she was near, my eyes watered. Uncle Henry said she was probably wearing all that perfume to disguise the whisky on her breath. That made sense as she was a recent widow at the time. But I'm inclined to think my relative was making up another one of his stories, particularly as his history with her as a student had been no better than mine. Anyway, on the night of the Martian invasion she came dripping in lavender and carrying her Pekinese, a loathsome creature with bulging eyes and a tendency to yap at clouds, grass and everything in between. It was yapping as I opened the door.

"Quiet, Lancelot," said Mrs. Duncan. She brazened her way across the threshold and, ignoring me, followed the sound of voices as they escaped from the living room. Before I could close the door behind her, more neighbors poured in. Some of them were worried about the broadcast, but others came because they thought we were throwing a party.

By the time Dad arrived from the station, the celebration was in full swing. The cookies had disappeared and Mom was in the kitchen making sandwiches.

"What in tarnations?" were my Dad's first words when he found Mom in the kitchen.

Mrs. Duncan and her Pekinese had followed my parent into the kitchen when she saw him arrive. Normally the area was reserved for the privacy of the family, but being a teacher who'd taught over half the population, she didn't stand by convention. "Well, John, what about these invaders? Is there a plan?"

With one hand rubbing the back of his neck, Dad turned to acknowledge his former teacher. "Blamed if I know, Mrs. Duncan. Elsie says we're almost out of bread."

"Do you intend to feed them?"

"I don't see how we can avoid it, being as they're in our living room."

"T-The living room?" Mrs. Duncan's jaw dropped as if coming to a sudden understanding. "Are you saying they can invade our bodies? Look like us?"

"Who?"

"The Martians, of course!" Mrs. Duncan glared at my father as if he'd stumbled over the words, 'Run Spot, Run.'

Once he understood her, a thin smile curved across his face. After twenty-seven years, he seemed to think he'd finally gotten the better of his former nemesis.

"Mrs. Duncan, haven't you and the others been listening to the radio? There aren't any Martians. It was a Halloween prank cooked up by some actor named Orson Welles. I'm surprised you were taken in. The idea's pretty farfetched, don't you think?"

Mrs. Duncan looked as if the ground had caved in under her but she refused to blink. "Of course it's farfetched, John," she began slowly, "but in my several years of experience, there are some who will believe anything. Your duty, don't you think, is to inform your guests?"

That said, Mrs. Duncan quick-marched from the kitchen with my father in tow. I couldn't help noticing his bowed head. He looked as if he were on his way to the principal's office. It reaffirmed then what I already knew. You can't argue with a teacher.

A short while later, Mom and I heard a mixture of laughter and argument coming from the living room. Most people were relieved by what Dad had told them, but a few insisted that maybe there was no hoax.

"Maybe it's a government cover-up," Mr. Dimwitty shouted. Uncle Henry agreed and so did a few others. But when they had time to think about it, most people concluded that if Arthur

Dimwitty and Henry Westerlund were on the same side, the idea was plain crazy. Soon after, everyone went home, some of them with red faces, and our bread crisis was averted.

As I said, my inspiration for playing a prank on Herman came from that phony Martian invasion, but it wasn't until a few days before the Halloween of 1939, that I was ready for action. I'd like to say it was a dark and stormy night when it all began, but it wasn't. Ohio was having one of those late Indian Summers when the evenings were balmy and a person could leave the windows open to catch a breeze. In a way, that was good. The mild weather made it more likely that little green men could be climbing in and out of windows to find subjects for their outer space experiments. Anyway, that was my story on the night when I shook Herman from a sound sleep.

"What is it? Whatdya want?" he snapped, refusing to open his eyes. "Let me sleep, can't ya?"

Ignoring him, I bent low to his ear. "What did they do to you, Herman? Are you hurt? Can you talk?"

"Whatdya mean, 'Can I talk?' I'm talkin' aint I?" By now his eyes had clicked open.

"What's that you said? Speak English, can'tcha?"

"I am speakin' English, ya fool!"

I shook my head. "Nope. Can't make out a thing you say. Is that Martian? Are they teaching you to talk like them?"

Herman shot up in his bed with his hair sticking out at right angles.

"Maybe I should get you a glass of water of something," I went on. "Maybe that would help."

"Help what? What are you playing at, Ollie? I know you're up to somethin'."

I took a step backwards as though he'd hissed at me. "Calm down, will you? I'm trying to help. Maybe you should go back to sleep. Yeah, maybe you'll make sense in the morning. I'm hoping you won't look so weird, either."

I backed away, keeping my eyes on him until I reached my bed. Then I curled into a ball as if trying to hide under my blankets. Herman sat watching me for a couple of minutes. Finally he thumped his pillow to make a dent for his head and rolled into it. "Blamed fool," he muttered.

In the morning, Herman quizzed me about my behavior of the previous night, but I acted as if he had been hallucinating. "I wouldn't talk too much about what you dreamed or imagined," I told him. "You don't want people thinking you're getting peculiar like Uncle Henry."

The second night it took my kid brother a little longer to settle down but eventually I heard him snuffling, a sure sign that he was deep in his dreams. That's when I started to shake him again.

"Herman! Wake up, will you? I can't take much more of this. Where've you been? What's going on?"

My kid brother shot up, his face drained of color. "What is it? What's happening?"

"You tell me," I answered. "I'm not the one floating out the window and disappearing into the night. Leastwise, you're talking so's I can understand you. Where're they're taking you? What do they want?"

''Who? Who's taking me?"

"Those little green men, of course. Martians... with big eyes, spindly arms and legs and green all over. Don't you remember?"

Herman's face crumpled as if he'd bitten into a broccoli sandwich. "Course I don't remember. I ain't been floatin' out of any windows. Maybe it's you who's having a bad dream or turning peculiar. Leave me alone or I'll tell Mom what you're up to."

I was surprised by my little brother's confidence. Maybe I'd played one trick too many on him. In any case, he turned his back on me and resettled under his covers. Disappointed, I glared down at his spiky hair and wondered what to do next. For sure, he wasn't going to believe he'd been kidnapped by Martians. Not on my say-so. He'd need proof.

Okay then, I'd give it to him even if I spent the rest of the night thinking about it, which I did. Morning found me with eyes as bloodshot as if they'd been filled with sand. But I was happy. My kid brother was going to get the scare of his life.

When he got home from school that afternoon, Herman ran off to play at Derrick's house. That gave me time to assemble my tools: a glass of pond scum, a flashlight wrapped in green tissue paper, tinsel and a comb with a square of writing paper for a makeshift kazoo. With all my props assembled, I could hardly wait for bedtime.

Fortunately, the rest of the day did not weigh heavily on my hands. Mrs. Wyerick, my sixth grade teacher, dropped-by the house to see if Mom would bring a cake as well as her famous pumpkin cookies to the school's Halloween carnival the next night. She sat in the kitchen, drinking coffee from the mug Mom handed her and talking about the haunted house that was going to be added this year, along with the traditional apple dunking booth and assorted hoop toss games. And of course, there would be lots and lots of food, she said laughing.

Watching her, I had to admit that Mrs. Wyerick was as different from Mrs. Duncan as a goat from a race horse, though they were about the same age and both strict. Mrs. Wyerick was tall and thin. with iron grey hair and a pair of blue eyes that were luminescent behind her metal rimmed glasses. Except for the fact that she gave too many geography quizzes, I liked her.

"No need to run wild in the streets this year, Oliver," she said, ruffling my hair. "Everything will be laid out at Madison."

I had to admit that on Halloween, my elementary school made a lot of effort to keep us kids out of mischief; but it was never entirely successful. Sooner or later the lure of the streets, where there was no adult supervision, took hold. We'd drift off in clumps as ghosts and goblins to terrorize our neighbors with the threat of "Trick or Treats." We were always expected and as if by magic our pillowcases filled to the brim with Carmel corn, Tootsie Rolls and candied apples. One exception was at the home of our dentist, Dr. Welch. He and his wife gave out carrot and celery sticks. Most kids skipped their house, but Mom insisted that Herman and I weren't to hurt their feelings; so we always came home with a fistful of vegetables.

As I sat in the kitchen listening to Mom and Mrs. Wyerick talk about the upcoming carnival, it was hard to say which event I was looking forward to most -- Halloween or the prank I was about to play on my little brother. Happily, I didn't have to choose. Each chiming of the hall clocked assured me that time was carrying me closer to both.

Though it wasn't dark outside yet, my brother and I were sent to bed at 8 pm. Mom said she didn't want us to get over-tired on Halloween and that an extra hour of rest would do us no harm. I don't know how she expected us to sleep with the sun practically shining in our faces. Herman complained as much.

Normally, I'd have raised my voice with his. But not that night. On that night I climbed the stairs with a light step and after giving a nod to my wash cloth, I fell into bed. Herman wasn't ready for his pillow, not with the sun painting yellow and red ribbons on the clouds. He dawdled over everything: brushing his teeth, washing behind his ears, getting into his pajamas... Part of me grew impatient, but another part knew that no good would come of trying to hurry him. He'd get suspicious. Already, he'd warned me that if I woke him up in the middle of the night with talk about little green men, he'd march into our parent's room and tell them what I was up to. My best strategy was to pretend to fall asleep. Eventually Herman settled down and before long I heard him snuffling in his dreams.

Unfortunately, it wasn't yet 9 o'clock. The adults were still up, talking in the kitchen, while Mom finished her baking. I didn't dare try anything until everyone was asleep.
The hands of the hall clock weren't my friends that night. I swear racers in a photograph moved faster. Finally, though, Uncle Henry came up the stairs, lumping at his customary pace, two stairs at a time. Dad followed soon after. But a century seemed to pass before Mom's light tread could be heard on the steps. She paused on the landing and opened the door to our room, which was her habit, and after satisfying herself that all was well, closed it again. Half an hour later, the house fell silent.

I must have fallen asleep because I awoke with a start when the hall clock struck eleven. My first inclination was to stay buried under the covers, as I felt warm and drowsy; but I'd made too many preparations to call everything off. Eventually, I sat up and listened for sounds of wakefulness. Everywhere it was quiet. Even the basement spiders appeared to be sleeping.

Most of my equipment lay under my pillow. The pond scum was hidden in the water glass under my bed. I got up and smeared most of its contents over Herman's pillowcase and a little on the lapels of his pajamas. I figured that if he went crying to Mom, she'd see it and think he'd puked. She might even give him a dose of cod liver oil, which would serve him right.

I followed up by scattering bits of tinsel everywhere; then I returned to bed and reached for my makeshift Kazoo. The vibrations tickled my lips as I blew into it, but I liked the eerie sound it made, particularly as I raised and lowered the pitch of my voice. What floated across the room might have been the dying moments of a goose or the braying of a mule with laryngitis or possibly the sound of an opera singer being strangled. However one described it, the noise was unnatural and it spooked my kid brother.

Herman rolled over in his bed and his face hit the green slime. "What the...?"

Now that I had his attention, I turned on my flashlight and made green, swirling circles on the ceiling. Reflections from the light hit the floor and window sill setting the tinsel afire.

"Cut that out, Ollie! It's not funny. And what's this stuff all over me. Mom's gonna be mad."

Herman sat dangling his legs over the side of his bed, ready to make a run for it. But he didn't move. His eyes were pinned to the floor, staring at the tinsel and trying to make out what it was.

What happened next came as a surprise to us both but it couldn't have suited me better. I'd seen it coming but let out a whoop when there was a thud against the window, as if it'd been hit with a sack of tomatoes. Herman, half convinced that Martians were after him, took a sling shot dive across the floor. "M-o-o-m," he wailed as he flew into the hall headed for our parent's room.

"They're here. They're here."

I'd never seen Herman so scared, not even when he was told he might need his tonsils taken out. He hadn't seen Bodacious Scurvy on the limb of the sycamore, hadn't witnessed the cat's failed attempt to leap through the half opened widow. My brother seemed convinced that the indignant yowls that pursued him were nothing less than the hunting cries of little green men.

He'd been gone for a couple of minutes before Dad flicked on the overheard light in our room, time enough for me to hide any evidence that might give me away.

"I-Is Herman all right?" I asked, faking a dazed expression.

Dad inspected the place before answering. "Anything funny going on in here, Oliver? I don't mean that cat howling outside."

"No, sir. I've been sound asleep."

"Sleep? How can anyone sleep with that cat making noise?" Dad stepped to the window and rapped on it to frighten the animal away. "Your brother's pretty scared," he said, turning to face me, thinks the Martians are after him. Know anything about that?"

"No sir."

"You'd better not. Anyway, your mother's giving him a dose of cod liver oil. When he comes back I don't want to hear a peep out of either of you. Got that?"

"Yes, sir," I answered. And he didn't. Halloween morning was a day just as it should be. The temperature had dropped to a crisp 33 degrees and painted the windows with frost. As it was bound to be a cold night for trick or treating, Mom pulled out the long johns and insisted that Herman and I wear them under our ghost sheets.

Herman didn't seem excited about Halloween. He was sullen at breakfast, didn't eat much and glared at me with daggers in his eyes. He knew I was responsible for the scare he'd gotten, but he couldn't prove it. Nor did he understand how I'd pulled off that bang at the window. He sat brooding while Mom went over the arrangements for the evening with Uncle Henry. Dad had to work at the station that night and Mom was serving as a volunteer at the school. Uncle Henry would be responsible for getting my brother and me to the carnival.

"I've got cold cuts for supper and you can heat up some soup so the boys will have something warm before they go out. Now don't be late, Henry. You head for the school around 6 o'clock and I want everyone home by 9. I'll be back some time later, after I help with the clearing up. I want the boys in bed as soon as they get home, if you can manage it."

"I'll manage it."

"Because John won't be home until midnight." Mom went on as though Uncle Henry hadn't said a word.

"Elsie, will you not excite yourself anymore? I know what to do. Relax."

"Well if you're sure..."

"I'm sure."

Mom looked at Uncle Henry as if the feeling wasn't mutual, but said no more about the evening arrangements.

When the hall clock struck 6 p.m. Herman and I were standing in the living room in our sheets. Uncle Henry didn't keep us waiting. He liked Halloween, too. This night, unlike most years, he wasn't wearing a costume, though. His habit, in the past, had been to hide in the porch shadows and when kids came to ring our door bell, he'd leap out dressed as a warlock or a werewolf.

Everyone knew he was in hiding, but he was rewarded with screams of delight, all the same. Maybe because he was in charge that evening, he'd decided to look normal, dressed as he was in the hat Mom had bought him, a pair of Levis and his plaid mackintosh.

After examining our costumes to make sure they weren't too long, he handed us our empty pillowcases for trick or treats and we headed for school. I was so excited that I jogged ahead of the other two. Normally, Herman would try to keep up, given his competitive nature, but that night he lagged behind, his hand tucked into Uncle Henry's. As I looked back, I noticed how small he was and that he had to hop two steps for every one taken by the man in the mackintosh. Now and again, he'd look up at his uncle as if for reassurance. I guess my hoax had scared him more than I had expected.

To be honest, Herman always was a puzzle. He was born when I was almost 5, so I didn't know what to make of him. I wasn't used to having another kid around. Mostly I saw him as a nuisance or someone to tease. But as I watched him totter along under his sheet that evening, I realized that in some way, I'd grown used to the little guy. I couldn't imagine life without him. I regretted my prank and promised myself to make it up to him -- share half my Halloween candy or if I won a prize at the hoop toss, I'd give it to him.

With my conscience put to rest, I ran toward Stubby, Luscious and the rest of the gang the minute we reached the school yard. Together we moved among the tide of witches, pirates and things-that-go-bump-in-the-night with our hearts in high spirits and our voices earsplitting. This was no time to be ladies and gentlemen. This was a night for being blindfolded at the haunted house, for having our hands dunked in bowls of cold spaghetti and peeled grapes and for being told that our fingers were churning in goblin guts and goblin eyeballs.

By 7:30 p.m. most of us had dunked for apples, heard our fortunes told and eaten our fill from tables laden with cakes and cookies. Our bellies groaned and yet we all agreed we needed to seek fresh blood.

And so, despite the hopes of our teachers but with the blessings of our parents, we drifted into the night like bats, each of us with our empty pillowcases.

Herman stood in the school yard watching me disappear, his hand still in Uncle Henry's. Unlike other Halloweens, he hadn't insisted on tagging along. I kept looking back to see if he'd change his mind. When he didn't, I felt disappointed, as if I were leaving a piece of myself behind.

"Tomorrow, I'll make it up to him," I vowed. Then I ran to catch up with the gang, which included Angel McBride, a girl in our class who sometimes substituted as a player during our baseball games. She was so polite on each doorstep, thanking and re-thanking everyone for their treats that she slowed us up. I was afraid I'd be home late because of her.

Happily, that wasn't the case. The hall clock was chiming 9 p.m. as I tiptoed through the front door, my pillowcase slung over my back. It felt strange to come home to a house that was dark and quiet. In the past, the windows would be ablaze with light and the family would be waiting as Herman and I stormed into the hall. But on that night, everything was different.

On the landing at the bottom of the stairs, I found a note from Uncle Henry. It said he'd gone to bed, being worn out from so much responsibility, and that I wasn't to switch on the bedroom light or do anything to wake Herman. My brother wasn't feeling well, the note said.

Quiet as a shadow, I entered our room, shoved the pillowcase under my bed and climbed between the sheets. To be honest, I wasn't feeling too chipper myself. My stomach was churning.

Mom's pumpkin cookies were laying siege to the Tootsie Rolls and the candied apple I'd devoured. Now all of them seemed to be tossing in a sea of green slime. Glad to be home, I must have drifted off the moment my head touched the pillow. How long I slept, I don't know, but I remember dreams about headless horsemen and giants chasing me through rivers of chocolate and mountains of gum drops and that I tripped over countless jelly beans as I tried to escape.

When I awoke it was to a noise that left me confused as to its origin. Was it of the real world or the cry of some demon pursuing me to the edge of my dreams? I sat up and to my satisfaction, discovered that the house was still. Whether it was midnight or the wee hours of the morning, I couldn't be sure for the drapes were drawn across the window and no light cracked under the bedroom door. I could barely make out my hand in front of my face. All I knew was that it was still night.

I sat for a moment trying to decide whether or not to return to my nightmares or wait out the dawn. Both choices were unappealing, but there wasn't much else to do. With Herman being sick, I had to be quiet. That's when I heard the noise again. The moan or sigh went on for a couple of seconds, long enough to assure me that I hadn't been dreaming the first time. Herman might have been snoring or passing gas, but the sound was like neither of those.

Another period of silence followed. Finally, I assured myself that nothing was amiss and feeling cold, I settled back under my covers, ready to risk another dream about giants. Then I heard it again -- that sigh or moan -- louder this time. Instinctively, I slung my head over the side of the bed and looked to see if Bodacious Scurvy, having his own set of bad dreams, might have been curled there. The space appeared to be empty, except for my pillowcase. What then had I heard? Was the wind playing tricks with the sycamore? But there was no wind. Had Uncle Henry left the radio playing downstairs? No, it wasn't on when I came home. Throughout, the house was silent. The stirring, unworldly and unidentifiable, was... in... my... room.

When I heard the sound a fourth time, my hands, my armpits turned clammy and my heart pounded like a tin drum. The presence, whatever it was, could be heard but not seen. I decided it was time to wake my little brother, no matter what Uncle Henry had written. Whether my intention was to save him or to share my fright, I don't know, but before I could put one foot upon the ground, a specter rose before me.

What I saw was a faint glow, green in color, radiating from Herman's side of the room and though he was still reclining with his eyes closed, he appeared to be hovering, like a magician's assistant, a good three inches above his bed with his blankets draped at his sides. As the distance between himself and his mattress seemed none too great, I tried to persuade myself that the flashlight or candle or whatever it was he might be holding was helping to create the illusion that he was afloat. But anyone with eyes could see that Herman's arms were at his side. Not only was he not the source of any light but he seemed blissfully unaware of his elevated condition.

He hovered a few seconds while I attempted to rationalize what I saw. Then with a jerk, his body rose to a distance not less than four feet above the ground and, to my horror, began to levitate in my direction. Closer and closer he came until reason flew out the window and my lungs swelled with terror.

"HERMAN. HERMAN. WAKE UP. HOLY MOLEY, WAKE UP WILL YA?" My words seemed to burst through the top of my cranium and I remember being so frightened that I continued to scream a second or two after the overhead light flicked on. Mom was standing in the doorway, dressed in her hat and coat, breathless from having dashed up the stairs.

What must she have thought when she found not lions and tigers and bears, but her two sons and Uncle Henry? Her brother, no doubt, posed the biggest shock. A flashlight, wrapped in green tissue paper, jutted from his mouth and he was dressed like a burglar, all in black, including his face which had been shoe polished. His youngest nephew he held suspended in his arms, looking stiff as a board and blinking sheepishly. After that, the sight of her eldest son standing in his bed, having peed in his pajamas, must have seemed ordinary. She addressed none of us at first, but stepped to the window and threw it open.

"It's all right, everyone. Henry's had another bad dream."

With the neighbors mollified, she closed the window and turned toward her family with eyes ablaze.

"You're s-s-o-o lucky John isn't here," she said to my uncle,

"And you boys would be punished for sure..."

"Me?" I objected. "What have I done?"

"Quiet, Oliver. And Henry, you'd be shipped off to Enid's for another vacation."

"Aw Elsie, it was a joke. It's Halloween."

"Don't 'Aw, Elsie' me! You said you could be trusted..."

"And I could. The boys are home, safe and sound, aren't they?"

"You call scaring your nephew witless, being trustworthy? Just look at him?" Suddenly, Mom snapped her head in my direction.

"Get out of those pajamas, Oliver, and bring me a new set of sheets. I expect you've made a mess of everything. And you two," she swung round to glare at Herman and Uncle Henry again, "You're going to make his bed. That's the least you can

83

do."

Once the three of us were alone, Herman and Uncle Henry started giggling. They couldn't have been more pleased with themselves if they'd spun straw into gold. Of course, I took no part in their levity. I slumped against a far wall with my arms folded. He was tucking up the last corner of my bed sheet when the man in black face looked over at me.

"Aw, come on, Ollie. Don't be mad. If anyone can appreciate a joke, you should. Anyway, you had it coming. Don't play tricks unless you can take 'em too."

I started to object. "But your trick was..."

"Better. Yeah, I know." He gave me one of his crooked grins. "But I got a consolation prize for you and your brother if you forgive me."

"What is it?" I asked warily. "Donkey do-do?"

Uncle Henry headed to our closet. He pulled out a paper sack that was lying on the floor and dumped its contents on to the center of my bed. When we saw it, Herman and I shouted, "Mars bars!"

Chapter 7 - Passing Through

Photograph: *Albert Branscomb and John beside the attic
window they've just repaired, November 1939*

In 1939 when I was eleven, the ladies of our church vanished
for two days, as they always did in mid-winter. They gathered
at a nearby farm to plan their charitable activities for the
upcoming year. Reverend Bolstrand was the only man allowed
on the premises. Every other male parishioner was barred and
so came to dread the occasion as it meant two days without
bread rising on the windowsill or the hope of a hot evening
meal. Adding to these deprivations was the inconvenience of
having to keep tabs on the young. Bereft of their teachers, all of
them of the vanished gender, the children had to be supervised
by their fathers or brothers or uncles. Still, the disappearance
was tolerated, as the ladies were in engaged in a benevolent
cause.

A few unmarried men voiced their discontent on occasion, in
the barber shop or the pool hall where the majority of those
present was likely to agree. But on a day in January, when the
temperature was so cold even the thermometers seemed to have
frozen, our postman, Mr. Hartley, stumbled into the Marabar
diner, ordered a slice of hot apple pie and astounded everyone
with his pronouncement that the ladies' two day retreat was a
Strike and probably illegal.

Mr. Hartley was a man half the size of his wife, so no one
would have imagined him capable of much courage; yet his
complaint, voiced in all male company, brought a gleam of

85

respect into the eyes of the men who were lined up like birds on a telephone line at the counter. No one made a reply, though. They stared into their mugs as if they could stir their coffee with their eyes. One or two did glance in my dad's direction, where he sat in a booth opposite me. Being a town constable, they must have wondered if he had an opinion, which he didn't because he kept pouring ketchup on his fries as if he hadn't heard a word.

Oscar, the proprietor of the Marabar, was the one to break the silence. He was flipping burgers at his grill behind the service window. "Well, I don't know what you'd call it," he bellowed, so everyone in the room could hear, "but it's rumored those gals do a lot more than talk charity when they get together. I hear they sometimes talk politics. Can you believe it? Why I bet most of 'em don't even know who the governor is!"

The remark got one of the pig farmers riled up. "Pshaw! You think that's bad? Last year, my wife came home from one of those gatherings and declared Hester ought to go to college. Said our daughter was bright enough to have a career. Now, isn't that the damnedest thing? Tell me what good college would do? No good! Just make an old maid of her."

"Hester couldn't be stupid enough to want to go to college," snorted the second pig farmer seated beside him.

"I sure in hell hope not," replied the first.

"Trouble is, lots of women are thinkin' of movin' into places they don't belong," said a sandy haired man, three stools down from Mr. Hartley. "One of these days, some lady doctor's gonna hang a shingle right here on Main Street. Imagine havin' to go to her for a... a..." Here the man cleared his throat as if to speak in confidence, "... a physical?" A visible shudder went up among the men clad in Levis.

Mrs. McBride, the red-haired widow who waitressed at the

diner six days a week, stopped wiping the counter in front of her. Jabbing a delicate fist into one hip, she glared at the farmer who'd spoken. "I don't see anything wrong with that. Women go to male doctors all the time."

"Aw, that's different," rejoined the sandy haired man. "Men know what they're doin'."

"And women don't?"

Realizing his mistake, the man's voice took on an apologetic whine. "I'm only sayin' what everybody knows, Pat. Women get too emotional over things..."

"Too emotional? What are you afraid of, Homer? That some lady doctor'll get too emotional over your privates?"

Homer's cheeks turned cherry red as the men around him, his former allies, broke ranks and collapsed into laughter. "She's got ya there," said one, slapping his friend on the back.

"Never mind," bawled another, "your privates aren't big enough to worry about."

After that, Homer quieted down and talk turned to the weather, a safer subject and one of endless fascination to the men whose lives depended upon it.

That night I lay in bed listening to my brother, Herman, snore and thinking about what I'd heard at the Marabar. I had to agree with the men: the female half of the human race followed a logic that could leave the other half stupefied. My mother was no exception. One minute she'd be after her brother, my Uncle Henry, to clean up his room, then in another she'd defend his mess if my dad had the temerity to complain. Of course, back then I was a boy and knew little about how a woman could touch a man's heart and sometimes leave him sadder and wiser; at least not until I made the acquaintance of Albert Warren

Branscomb in November 1939.

The day we met, the sky was cloudy and the scent of a fresh snow hung in the air. I was on an errand to the hardware store. We needed boards to cover a window that had broken in the attic, which was Uncle Henry's room. Uncle Henry had had one of his altercations with Bodacious Scurvy. The cat had sought shelter amidst the piles of old newspapers and rags that my uncle counted among his "treasures."

The day was Saturday and nearing suppertime. I was in a hurry but as I passed my elementary school I saw smoke curling from the woods behind the building. Was dear old Madison burning, I half-hoped? My geography report was due on Monday, and until then, I hadn't given it a thought.

To investigate would delay my errand, but I took a detour anyway, crossing the playground and heading for the column of smoke, about fifty yards in the distance. At the wood's edge, I crouched low to the ground like an Indian tracker, not knowing what I would find and thinking it never hurt to be cautious.

Not far into the shadow of the trees I saw him, a man seated before a campfire with his back to me. He wore a plaid cap pulled down over his ears and his coat, a dirty pea green, was pulled away at the seams as if he'd outgrown it, or it was somebody's cast off. He heard my footfall and turned.

"You saw the smoke? I was hoping that if I kept the fire small..."

The minute he spoke, I knew he wasn't from around home. New York, maybe, or Boston. Somewhere foreign. But I liked his face. He wasn't handsome exactly, but his broad features made him seem open, like a man you could trust. I didn't hesitate to accept his invitation to join him on the log he'd placed before the fire. Then he pointed to the enamel pot hanging above the flames. "Coffee? You take it black, I hope."

"I take it anyway it comes," I replied, trying to sound like my dad when he'd swing one leg over a stool at the Marabar counter. The truth was I'd never been offered coffee before. My parents thought I was too young. But the man beside me didn't seem to think that being twelve was an impediment. He handed me an enamel cup and as we sat, he talked about a raft of things: the coming war, his time as a volunteer with the British Army, about the shrapnel lodged in his legs at Dunkirk and how the doctors said it couldn't be removed. He'd been sent home and had been riding the rails for several months trying to find somewhere to feel comfortable.

I couldn't help but admire the man so I told him about our town and he said it sounded like a nice place to live. We basked in comfortable silence together for a while and then I asked him what sort of work he thought he could do. That's when I almost fell off the log. Albert Warren Branscomb told me he was a physicist with a degree from Harvard University.

The idea of a person of such learning having to ride the rails might seem incredible today, but during the depression and its aftermath, many men had been deprived of a decent living and so they crisscrossed the country by box cars looking for work. Albert was not the first itinerant I'd seen and maybe not the most educated either. But by 1939, the economy had improved and if he'd wanted to, I suspect that he could have found a place to settle down. Maybe he wasn't ready. Maybe he'd seen too much of the war in Europe. One thing for certain, though, he was a good storyteller. I must have sat for nearly an hour mesmerized by his tales. That's why, when the church bells struck the half hour, I leaped up from where I was sitting like my pants were on fire.

"My gosh! I gotta get to the hardware store or my dad'll skin me!" I told him what had happened at home and how we had to put a couple of boards across the window until we could hire someone to fix it on Monday.

Albert stood up with a gleam in his eye. "No need to wait till then," he said. "I can glaze a window. What size is it?" Without thinking, I gave Albert the dimensions Dad had given me for the boards.

He grunted in satisfaction then doused his fire with the remains of the coffee. "Come on, Oliver. I'll have new glass in that hole before your mother can put biscuits on the table." He paused to squint down at me. "She is a good cook, isn't she?"

"The best," I told him.

Albert Warren Branscomb looked to be in a good mood as we headed home from the hardware store. He took long strides and seemed eager to meet my parents. I, on the other hand, given time to think about the presence of a hobo in our living room, had slowed my steps to a snail's pace. From time to time, Albert got so far out in front of me that he had to turn back to ask if he was headed in the right direction.

My dad was standing in the hallway waiting for me as Albert and I burst through the front door. The look on his face when he saw a hobo was everything I had imagined and more. Albert, fortunately, didn't seem to notice. He stuck out his hand for my dad to shake.

"Your son says you need a window fixed. As it happens, I'm a glazier, so I came along to help."

Dad stood stiff as a cigar store Indian and said nothing. "I'm not asking for pay," Albert went on, "Just a hot meal and maybe a garage where I could sleep for the night. It's pretty cold outside."

By now my mother had wandered in from the kitchen to see who the stranger was.

She was carrying a dish towel in one hand and attempting to

smooth a lock of her blonde hair with the other. Albert flashed a smile that made her cheeks go rosy. I was surprised by that. Albert was tall and broad shouldered, it's true. But so was my dad, except that Dad didn't have Albert's shock of blonde hair. His hair was brown and thinning. I was glad that Mom seemed to approve of my new friend and especially glad when, after she'd learned why he'd come, she invited him to stay for supper. With a deal struck, my dad found his tongue and told Albert that if he didn't mind, there were some empty beds at the jail where he could spend the night. The offer didn't offend my friend in the least and so the two men headed up the stairs toward the attic. Before long, we could hear a tap, tap tapping and the voices of my dad and Albert in conference.

Herman had stumbled into the kitchen with sleep in his eyes almost as soon as the noise began. He wanted to know about the racket, but Mom ignored the question and told him to get cleaned up as we had a guest for supper. She was pouring flour into a bowl at the time, as I'd happened to mention that Albert was partial to biscuits. Naturally, Herman didn't budge.

"Who is it?" he said, jamming his elbows into the counter as Mom cut ice cold butter into the flour. "Is it Uncle Henry?"

"Of course not. Uncle Henry's on the bus to Columbus. You remember. He's going to stay with Aunt Enid for a while."

"Yeah, I remember. Dad took him to the station."

"Your father doesn't blame Uncle Henry for the window, if that's what you mean. It was that cat. I don't know how that animal keeps finding its way into the attic."

"Maybe Uncle Henry lets him in."

Mom stopped kneading her dough to glare at me. "Now why would he do that? He doesn't even like cats."

"Maybe he's lonely."

"With family around?"

"I think he'd rather have a dog," Herman muttered.

By the time Dad and Albert descended the stairs, the kitchen was drenched in edible aromas. Both men headed for the sink to wash up. I was relieved to see the smile on Dad's face.

"Albert's done a fine job, Elsie. You need to look at it after supper, which smells awful good, I might add." These were the first cheerful words Dad had uttered since quarreling with Uncle Henry that morning.

Mom pretended not to hear him and kept her eyes on the chicken she was frying. "Oliver, the biscuits are ready. Take them out of the oven. Everyone else, go sit at the table."

The crispness in her voice made everyone snap to attention, everyone except Albert who stood beside the oven door taking in the scent of freshly baked biscuits.

"Those sure smell great," he said, shaking his head in disbelief at his good fortune. "I expect your son wasn't exaggerating when he said you were the best cook in the county."

Mom blushed for a second time that afternoon. "Well, I wouldn't go so far as to say that. Maybe it's been too long since you've had a home cooked meal."

"You'd be right about that, Mrs. Larson. But there's nothing wrong with my memory. I know good cooking when I smell it. I'm just grateful to be here today."

"Well thank you, Albert. And please, call me Elsie."

Dad soon realized that the peace he enjoyed at the supper table could be laid at Albert's door, and so he seemed to have a change of heart about carting him over to the jail once the meal was over.

"What do you think, Elsie," he said, as he stood at the kitchen window watching the snow fall in drifts. "Shall we let him stay in Henry's room? Just for the night?"

"I'll have to lay out fresh sheets," Mom replied, in a tone that suggested she was pleased with Dad's decision. "It won't take long. Herman can help."

The next morning, my little brother and I awoke to the smell of bacon frying. Both of us bolted upright in our beds. "I love Sundays," said Herman, his hair sticking out like a fan.

We headed for the kitchen in our bare feet, still wearing our pajamas. Dad was right behind us, but he wore Levis and a pullover as it was his day off. Mom stood at the stove flipping pancakes.

"Everything smells so good, I could almost imagine it was our anniversary. You made pigs in a blanket, too?"

"I want Albert to have a good meal and something to take with him if he really needs to go."'

Dad scratched his head. "What do you mean, 'if he really needs to go'?"

"I mean, he's such a nice man. Well educated..."

Herman looked up at our father. "Yeah, Dad, can we keep him? Can we keep Albert?"

"'Mr. Branscomb' to you, Herman," Dad corrected. Then his hand fell to the back of his neck as if he were experiencing a sharp pain. "Elsie, haven't we got enough extra mouths to..."

I didn't have to see my mom's face to know this reference to her brother had brought fire to her eyes. My dad saw it too, how she went stiff and stopped turning the pancakes. Herman didn't notice anything. He went on insisting that Mr. Branscomb wanted to be called Albert. He'd said so... last night... at the supper table. Herman looked around. "Hey, where is he anyway?" Isn't he up yet?"

"Oh, he's up all right," Mom answered. Her voice was still cold from my dad's affront. "He's been up for hours. Right now, he's out back stacking the wood, something I asked your father to do last week." That said, Mom took my little brother by the shoulders, herded him to the kitchen table and shoved him into his chair. "Oliver, ask Mr. Branscomb to come in, please."

At the table, we sat for a while in silence. Albert kept searching our faces for an explanation. Maybe he thought he had done something wrong. A couple of times he said how good everything tasted but that's as far as the conversation went until Dad decided to ease the situation.

"I hear there's a job going at the Humane Society, feeding the animals and cleaning out the cages. I could talk to the manager Monday, if you're interested. It doesn't pay a lot, but you could stay here until you get your first check. Elsie's brother won't be back for a couple of weeks. And besides, with two boys around there's always something to fix."

Albert put down his fork and stared at my dad as if he was unsure about what he'd heard.

"Of course, it's just a suggestion." My dad shrugged. "Maybe you'd rather not..."

"No, no. It's a fine idea. I just wasn't expecting ..."

Mom gave my dad a melting look, then assured Albert that in these difficult times people were supposed to help one another.

"Hooray!" Herman shouted his mouth full of pancakes. "Albert can show me those rope tricks he's been talking about."

I gave my brother a hard look. He seemed to have forgotten that Albert was my discovery.

Come Monday, Mrs. Wyerick sprang a geography test on my sixth grade class, and of course I wasn't prepared. With Albert around to tell his stories, the stuff in books seemed pretty tame. In a way, just listening to him was an education. But I knew Mrs. Wyerick wouldn't see it that way when she graded my test. I was pretty down in the mouth as Herman and I arrived home from school that day. We went to the kitchen like we usually did, but were surprised to find Albert under the sink, tapping on some pipes.

The scene was one of infinite fascination to Herman and me because Dad seldom worked with his hands. He might tinker with the police car engine, change the oil, or the filters, but beyond that he was at a loss. Someone tinkering with pipes was irresistible. Of course Mom tried to shoo us away, but Albert said he didn't mind having us around. Said he worked better with an audience. Then he asked Herman to hand him the wrench he'd found in the garage and Herman looked to be in hog heaven.

"Whatcha lookin' for?" he said as he crawled into the tight space to lie down beside Albert. Albert didn't answer at first. He was straining to turn the pipe. It came loose on the second twist and splattered the pair with rusty water and soap residue. Herman let out a squeal as he was not on friendly terms with either soap or water but Albert uttered a cry of satisfaction.

"Did you find it, Albert? Was it there?"

Mom sounded nervous so I had to ask. "What is it? What did you lose?"

Albert sat up with a smile breaking across his face. "Nothing, Oliver. She didn't lose anything." Then he dropped something round and gooey into Mom's hand. She held the mess to her cheek as if it were a blob of cold cream and I noticed tears shining in her eyes.

"I'll never take it off again. Never!"

At supper neither Herman nor I said anything about the wedding ring, mostly because Mom promised us an extra helping of apple pie if we didn't. Anyway, Dad was interested in how Albert did with his interview at the Humane Society. Albert told him it went well and that he was to start work the next day. He mentioned that on his way home he'd stopped to celebrate at Miss Ingrid's Bake Shoppe, and when she heard his story, she asked him to set up a few shelves for her that had been collecting dust in the store room.

"I got more than coffee and donuts," he said, jingling some coins in his pocket, "I owe that to you, Mr. Larson. Word seems to travel fast around here. People know what you're doing for me and apparently you have a lot of influence."

Dad looked pleased by the compliment but he didn't let it go to his head. "Just folk's respect for the law, that's all."

"Now you know that's not why people look up to you, John," Mom said, pouring Dad his second cup of coffee. "Everyone in this town knows you're a hero."

"Oh?" Albert dropped his fork onto his plate while his eyes formed a question.

My dad didn't say anything but Herman did. "Yeah, he shot some bank robbers once. Got a medal for it and everything. It's on the mantle in the living room. Wanna see it?" Herman was half way off his chair before Dad could put a hand on his shoulder to set him down again.

"Finish your supper, son. Albert can see it later, if he wants to."

After Herman and I had finished the evening dishes, we were sent to our room to do home work. We never did get to know if Albert saw the medal. I suppose that he did. Anyway, instead of attending to his sums, Herman leaned back in his chair with his hands clasped behind his head. "How come Albert's a hobo, Oliver? He ain't lazy or nothin.' He works hard."

"I know he does and he's smart, too. But when you weren't more than a baby, a lot of men rode the rails. They were looking for work on account of the depression. You don't remember, but one of 'em died right here in this town."

"Really?" Herman's eyes grew owl-like.

"Yep. Froze to death in the woods. That's why Reverend Bolstrand and the church ladies meet out at old Hooper's farm once a year. The farmer's got a couple of bunkhouses he don't use any more on account of he gave up on cattle ranching. So that's where the ladies plan for their charities. The men don't like the disappearance much but they don't want anyone to freeze to death, either. Or to see anybody go hungry."

"Yeah," said Herman, chewing the idea in his head slowly. "That would be terrible." A short period of silence followed before he spoke again. "But do ya think he'll stay now that he's got a job and all? It would be neat, wouldn't it? Mom and Dad really like him."

"Well, he can't stay here, if that's what you're thinking. What would we do with Uncle Henry? Have you forgot about him?"

From his blank expression it was clear that he had. "Maybe they could both stay in the attic. It's big enough and I bet Uncle Henry would like him. They're alike in a way. Different from most."

"We'll just have to see." I sighed as I turned back to my geography. "We'll just have to see."

Ten days went by before we heard from Aunt Enid about our uncle. He'd come down with the croup or something and wasn't fit for travel. During that time, Albert continued to occupy the attic and Dad seemed glad for some sensible male companionship and for the 3 dollars a week he received from our lodger for room and board. Mom didn't pine for her missing brother as much either, not with Albert around. He made her laugh and showered her with compliments. Sometimes, when he was teasing her, she looked like a young girl and I wondered why I'd never seen her that way before. Herman was happy, too. Albert taught him a couple of rope tricks that made a big hit at school.

But I wasn't too certain about our tenant. Sometimes he looked at my mom with soft eyes, the way my dad did, and then a shadow would fall across his face and he'd stare into the distance as if he were reminding himself about the sound of a train whistle or the feel of the wind blowing across his face from an open box car. I wasn't sure what that look meant, but it made me sad and I guessed at those moments that Albert was sad, too.

I shouldn't have been surprised when after three weeks with us Albert Warren Branscomb decided to leave. I was the first one he told. Despite the snow that powdered the ground, I'd been waiting on the porch for him to come home from the Humane Society. I wanted to show him the "B" I'd got on my math test, thanks to his coaching the night before. He looked at my score and swore he was as proud of me as a man could be and said that he was glad he'd been around to help. That's when he broke the news. He'd be hopping a train the next day. I know my face puckered because it took all my resolve not to cry.

Albert stared into the distance and looked embarrassed. "It's for the best, Oliver. Your mom and dad don't want me hanging around forever and your uncle'll be home soon."

"Aw, that's stupid!" I sputtered. "Everyone in this town likes you and if you'd give him a chance, Uncle Henry would like you, too. I know he would."

"Be that as it may, it's time." Though it was no more than a whisper, Albert's voice was firm.

I shook my head, unable to understand. "But why do you have to leave? Don't you like us? Is it me? H-have I done something wrong?"

Albert offered a thin smile. "My leaving's got nothing to do with you, Oliver. We're buddies and always will be."

"We can't be buddies if you're not here." My voice betrayed the hurt I was feeling and Albert reacted by pressing his hands on my shoulders and forcing me to look at him.

"Distance makes no difference between friends. I'll never forget you, Oliver, or your family's kindness to me. Truth is, you're more likely to forget me."

"Never!" I shouted as I broke free and turned my back on him. "I'll never forget you! Not EVER!"

Albert's hands took hold of my shoulders again. They were big and warm and comforting. "Well, that's good. It means we'll be buddies for a long, long time."

At the table that evening, everyone was quiet. We all knew that Albert was leaving and nobody liked it. Dad tried to be matter-of-fact about it. He asked Albert if he'd given his notice to the Humane Society, which he had, and if he knew where he might be headed. Albert jingled some coins in his pocket and said that he'd never been so rich but that he'd made no plans. Tomorrow, sometime, he'd hop a train going in any direction.

"But you'll write to let us know how you are doing, won't you?" The whole time Mom had hovered at his side like he was a sick child. "More biscuits, Albert? More gravy?"

He answered politely but his eyes never met hers. I got the feeling he was afraid that if they did, he'd break apart.

The next morning, I got up extra early so I could say goodbye, but Albert wasn't in the attic. I found him outside, clearing snow from the walk for the last time. Mom and Dad hadn't come downstairs yet.

"I've been waiting for you," he said, stopping to rest on his shovel. "How about skipping school today? Just you and me spending time together before I go."

My eyes lighted up when I heard that. "Ya mean it? Just you and me?"

"Just the two of us. I've got some things I'd like to show you. Maybe it'll help you understand why I have to go..."

I kicked at the snow to show that I'd never understand. "What if my folks won't let me? What then?"

"Then maybe we won't ask. We'll just do it. Anyway, it'll be educational. We're going to the library."

"The library! How's that better than bein' in school!"

"You'll be with me, for one thing. And it'll be fun for another. I want to show you pictures of the places I've been and the places I'd like to see someday."

"Sounds like a geography lesson to me."

"Come on, Oliver. Where's your spirit of adventure?" When I

remained silent, Albert decided to sweeten the deal. "Tell you what, if you think it's going to be boring, we'll stop at the Bake Shoppe afterwards and I'll buy you all the chocolate éclairs you can eat. Deal?"

That morning I spent with Albert Warten Branscomb was one of the most memorable in my life. It isn't as if we did anything special. Mostly we talked. And mostly we were at the library. Albert and I looked at a jillion books. Lots of them had pictures of the places he'd been -- some of them so small that they didn't appear on any maps. But he described them in such detail that they formed bright, shiny images in my mind like presents under a Christmas tree. And they were gifts, in a way, because they were images of worlds I'd probably never see -- like the cafe in White Fish, Montana that served a foot high stack of flap jacks and coffee so black you could see your face in it. I told him I wished Mrs. Wyerick could make her geography lessons half as interesting.

Albert leaned back in his chair with his arms akimbo. "Well, maybe she doesn't view the subject the way I do, Oliver. When I look at a map, like the one in front of us, I don't see wiggles and lines on a piece of paper. I see God's work: his mighty rivers and majestic mountains and all the people He created who praise his name. They don't use the same name for him, of course, but however they pray I'm reminded that this planet is a gift to us, one that we shouldn't squander. Think about geography that way, Oliver, and maybe you'll know to leave the world a little better than you found it."

He looked so serious staring down at me that a lump formed in my throat. I realized how much in my life I had taken for granted: my family, my education, and even my warm safe bed. But the world really didn't owe me anything. I had an obligation to the world. It was a sobering thought and the weight of it must have crumpled my expression because Albert let out a laugh that was round and full and hearty.

Miss Berenson, the librarian who'd been staring at me off and on, snapped her head in our direction. She was a stout woman in her early fifties, maybe. Her hair was turning gray but her skin was smooth as a baby's. According to my mom, Miss Berenson had been married once but when the union didn't last, she'd gone back to her maiden name, preferring to pass as a spinster rather than a divorcee. Anyway, Albert threw her a dazzling smile that made her blush and sent her back to her indexing.

"I surely love libraries," he sighed, once we had our privacy again. "They're magical places. Time machines, really."

"How do you mean?" I frowned. I hadn't finished digesting my obligation to the world and now Albert was talking about libraries and time machines.

The man beside me shrugged. "Look around you, Oliver. On these walls is the entire record of human and natural history. Why, you can go all the way back to the dinosaurs if you want."

I thought about that for a moment and then decided that maybe Albert didn't know everything. "Yeah, you can go back, but that don't make this place a time machine. You can't see into the future."

"What about Jules Verne?" he replied, casting a smug look in my direction. "You ever read him?"

"Aw, that don't count. That's fiction."

"What about those submarines and rockets. Didn't he give his readers a glimpse of the future?"

"Maybe, but nobody's gone to the moon."

"Could be they will, one day."

Albert's eye spied a copy of the National Geographic that was lying on a table nearby. On the cover was the picture of a grey wolf standing in the wilderness against a background of snow. "Look at that guy, will you? You just know he thinks he's king of the world."

"Think so?" I shrugged. "Looks more to me like he's lonely."

"Could be," Albert conceded. "But then, one man's loneliness can be another man's freedom. This wolf doesn't answer to anyone. He can do what he likes and go wherever the wind chases him."

"He can't walk up Main Street," I objected. "My dad would shoot him."

Albert roughed up my hair in a way that normally would have annoyed me. But coming from him, it didn't. "You know what I mean, don't you, Oliver?"

I nodded as tears welled into my eyes. All this talk about far away places and wolves wanting their freedom was Albert's way of saying goodbye. I was going to have to let him go. But I didn't want to. I tried to find the words to convince him to stay, but they wouldn't come on account of the ache in my throat.

"Come on, Oliver," Albert said, taking pity on me. Let's buy us some chocolate éclairs."

The clock on the Bake Shoppe wall read 3:15 in the afternoon as we entered. The place was empty at that time, so Albert and I were at our leisure to decide between chocolate éclairs or those cream-filled neapolitans with their filigree layers of crust or the deliciously white sugar cookies that were as big as my face. The decision proved too difficult, so we agreed to have some of each. When Miss Ingrid brought the order to our table, there was no mistaking our gluttony. Before us was a line of pastry as far as the eye could see. Albert looked sheepish. Miss Ingrid looked disapproving, but I was in hog heaven. The only problem was where to begin. I tucked in to a chocolate éclair and let the custard filling ooze down my chin. With an amused expression, Albert handed me a napkin. He wasn't eating anything. He seemed to enjoy watching me. The neapolitan came next and disappeared in no time. I was settling down to my first sugar cookie when Albert excused himself to go to the restroom. He ruffled my hair and I acknowledged his departure with a grunt, my mouth too full for words.

It wasn't until I heard the whistle of the four o'clock train that I looked up and realized that my friend had been gone for ten minutes or more. Miss Ingrid heard the whistle too, and come over to me with a bag of éclairs. Her eyes were moist with sympathy as she laid them, on the table face up, so that I could read the message written there.

"I'll never forget you, buddy."

My lips, my cheeks, my hands were sticky with granulated sugar... but the moment was bitter. Albert was on the four o'clock train. I knew it! And I also knew that I'd never see him again. Not ever. I couldn't help myself. I ran to the bathroom and threw up everything. "Damn you, Albert! Damn you, damn you, damn you!"

For months, I swore I'd never forgive Albert for the trick he'd played. It wasn't a proper goodbye. He'd taken the coward's way. He'd taught me so much, opened my eyes. I wanted to tell him... wanted him to know how much I loved him. But I knew I'd have never found the words. I was a coward just like him.

As I expected, we never saw or heard from our hobo again except once, a year after he'd gone. A package arrived from Anchorage, Alaska. Inside was a bottle of Tabu perfume for my mother and a book for me. On the cover page Albert had written the inscription:

"I'll never forget you, buddy."

I still have the copy: Jack London's, <u>*Call of the Wild*</u>.

Chapter 8 - Hudsons, Studebakers, and Fords... Oh My!

Photograph: *Herman, Oliver and Arthur Dimwitty standing by his red Oldsmobile, November 1939*

If the driving weather permitted, most Thanksgivings Aunt Enid and her husband, Dogget Herschel, came over from Columbus to celebrate with us. They'd occupy the attic and Uncle Henry would sleep on a cot in the room Herman and I shared. He didn't mind giving up his space to Aunt Enid. She was the oldest in the family, older than my mom by five years and older than he by seven. She'd always been kind to him, especially when both their parents, the Westerlund's, died suddenly of influenza.

Of course, the two younger children were almost grown up, Uncle Henry being 17 at the time and Mom already married with me on the way. Nevertheless, Aunt Enid fussed over both her siblings as if they were children. During the period of their parent's death, she held the family together, handling all of the affairs of the estate, such as they were.

Aunt Enid was the only member of the Westerlund family to have escaped our rural community to attend a secretarial and accounting school in Columbus. Once there, she rarely came home, except for a wedding or a funeral. She liked the big city and didn't seem to mind that she was unmarried as making her way in the world was satisfying. Eventually, she got a job as general office manager for the Herschel Studebaker Dealership and within a year the company's owner had proposed to her.

Our uncle-in-law would never have been taken for a salesman. He was a quiet man who wore an expression of surprise whenever he spoke, as though discovering his voice for the first time, each time. Aunt Enid swore that this monk-like silence was the secret to her husband's success in his business.

"Dogget has this knack for sizing people up before he quotes them a price on a new car," she liked to explain. "He asks them what they're willing to pay then waits. Doesn't say another word. Well, people get nervous when there's too much silence. Before long they're filling up the space with the story of their lives and when Doggett gets a good idea of their finances, he makes them an offer. Usually they're so surprised by the reasonableness of it, they drive home in a new automobile that same day. And why shouldn't they? My husband's a fair man."

Nobody argued with Aunt Enid's opinion of her husband. Everybody liked Uncle Herschel.

His being a car salesman was a point of great fascination to Herman and me because we were crazy about cars, any kind of car, Hudsons, Berlinas, Buicks, Cadillacs. We made a competition of who could recognize the makes and models of the automobiles going through town. We were pretty good at it, which surprised our dad who took little interest in machines of any kind. Once Uncle Herschel offered to sell him a Studebaker for the dealer's price, but Dad turned him down.

"This town's small enough to walk," he told his in-law. "And if the family heads for Florida to visit my folks, there's a bus and train depot to choose between." To be honest, Dad did have one other relative out of town, his younger brother Tom; but as he was with the navy somewhere in the Atlantic, Dad didn't feel a Studebaker would help much in getting to him.

"But if there's an emergency?" Uncle Doggett's black eyebrows rose higher than his voice.

108

Dad pointed his thumb in the general direction of the police station. "We got that 1935 Ford Sedan to take us to the outlying farms if there's a need. Mostly, though, it sits in the garage waiting for one of the guys to give it a wash and polish."

Dad's conviction that cars were an unnecessary expense and bother didn't seem likely to change, so Herman and I got our car expertise from hanging out at Daniel Maitland's repair shop from time to time. The place was really a blacksmithing operation in transition. The number of cars flowing through our main street on their way to Columbus or points west warranted the need for a garage, but the local demand was mainly for horseshoes and harness repair. Most of the outlying farmers hadn't converted to engines and still preferred to use horses to plough their fields. Nor was there much call for a mechanic from the residents of the town. Most of them didn't own cars. Dad was right. People could walk anywhere they needed to go.

Among the few residents crazy enough to drive a car in town was Arthur Dimwitty. He owned a 1934 Oldsmobile roadster, fire engine red with 8 cylinders. Even in winter he rode around with the top down, waving at his neighbors as he flew by. The car was his pride and joy. Some said his vehicle was the reason he was always made Grand Marshall of our Thanksgiving Parade. Others argued that it was because he was the town's only war veteran, having served as a cook under Admiral William Sampson during the Spanish-American War. No matter what the truth was, the roadster always brought a touch of class to the holiday procession. The rest of us who followed behind weren't much more than a ragtag bunch of gypsies.

Aunt Enid came to visit especially for the parade. Most of the town turned out, which allowed her to see her friends. It was one of those homey events where more people were marching in the street than cheering from the sidewalks. There was no fee, nor criteria for participation. Like attendance at a revivalist meeting, people behaved as the spirit moved them. The only thing organized was the Madison Elementary School Band which provided what could pass for music and was dominated by the sound of Harvey Erickson's tuba, an instrument that was about two feet taller than he was.

Herman and I usually rode our bikes behind the band, as did most of the other kids. Uncle Henry showed a few of us how to clothespin playing cards at right angles to our wheel spokes so that they made a fluttering noise when we pedaled. The riders thought the sound was music. Mrs. Hjalmer, a neighbor, said it sounded like a coven of deranged moths. Which ever was true, our bikes couldn't compete with the marching band whose job it was to lead everyone to the school and the volunteers who had stayed behind to lay out the community potluck. Only the lame or the infirm missed the event.

The parade of 1939 was a little different from those that had gone before, however. For some reason, that year Mr. Dimwitty said a few boys could ride with him in his roadster. He didn't specify who, so a bunch of us piled in. Herman and I squeezed into the front seat beside the driver, while Derrick dived into the back along with Stubby, Eric and Luscious, who took up space for two. It was a cram, but Mr. Dimwitty didn't have the heart to throw any of us out, so he took off down the road before anyone else decided to climb aboard.

I imagine that as Grand Marshall, he assumed that when he started to move everyone else would follow; but he was wrong. The flag bearer, Angel McBride, was late, so Mrs. Duncan, in charge of the parade, was in a flap and failed to notice that the roadster had set sail. We proceeded west in solitary splendor while a gaggle of on-lookers, who stood or sat by the side of the road, peered east in search of the rest of the marchers.

If Mr. Dimwitty failed to notice the absence of tuba notes in the air, it was no fault of his. True, he was hard of hearing, but the boys seated at his side and back were whooping like cranes as the wind swept through their hair. If a grenade had gone off in his path, he'd have been no wiser.

We had not traveled the length of three blocks before Derrick decided that he had to pee. He leaned over the seat and shouted into the driver's ear, "Are we there yet?" He meant how long would it be before we reached the school.

Mr. Dimwitty, responding to the urgency in the kid's voice, shouted back. "Don't worry. The end is near!"

"What's that, sir?" Derrick was having a hearing problem of his own because of our whooping and hollering. "Did you say we were almost there?"

"I said, 'The end is near'."

"Come again?"

"THE END IS NEAR!" The old man shouted his assurance several times as he drove down the street, a phrase which created confusion in the minds of many on-lookers. Several of them swiveled their heads east again, in search of the end of the parade, which was no more in evidence than its beginning.

About then, Mrs. Katafias, a cautious woman, grabbed her husband by the arm and started to run in the direction of home. Several others did the same. Perhaps they were remembering the 1906 San Francisco earthquake -- even though Ohio didn't have earthquakes. Or maybe it was the memory of Reverend Bolstrand's Sunday sermon where he accused our President, Franklin Delano Roosevelt, of trying to drag the country into war that set them off. Certainly the sight of our preacher high-tailing it up the main street while our only veteran proclaimed "the end is near," was enough to start a general panic. People took up the call, "the end is near," and began sprinting off in 180 directions.

Mom reported later that the stampede was widespread and when the parade finally did get started, Main Street looked like a ghost town. But in the car, we weren't concerned about stampedes. We were having the ride of our lives. No one complained when Mr. Dimwitty missed the turn off to the school and took a side road instead. He'd been looking into his rear view mirror at the time and was surprised to discover that the marching band was nowhere in sight. Well, to be honest, Derrick did start to point out the missed turn, but Stubby silenced him by putting his hand over the kid's mouth. And so we rode into the horizon, past dwindling numbers of shops and houses until we found ourselves surrounded by cornfields standing gaunt in the bright November afternoon.

By now our driver had figured out he'd missed the turnoff to the school and began looking for a widening of the road where he could pull the car around. None presented itself, however, and so we kept chasing the sun, stretching out our arms to catch the breeze like birds in flight. How long we might have continued in that direction, I don't know; but when Mr. Dimwitty caught sight of a dark speck looming larger and larger in his rearview mirror, the atmosphere changed. By craning our necks behind us, we could see it, a Ford sedan coming up fast. Then we heard the wail of a siren and knew we were in the sights of the town's police car.

Having nowhere to turn and wanting to get out of the way, Mr. Dimwitty gunned the gas, hoping to stay ahead of the on-coming vehicle long enough for it to reach the site of the emergency. It seemed like a good plan at the time as none of us realized that the emergency was us.

The roadster was clipping along at 45 miles an hour, a good pace on a country road, but it was no match for the sedan. The Ford was closing in with its siren blaring and a uniformed arm was waving to us from its open window. Mr. Dimwitty's face drained of color. He needed to make way, but how? Where?

Suddenly, he jerked the steering wheel into a sharp right turn and we shot off the road into a standing field of corn. With his foot still on the gas pedal, the old man leveled the stalks as if they were bowling pins. We bumped along for about a quarter of a mile, clinging to our seats to avoid being hurled from the car. We might have gone on a quarter of a mile more if the Oldsmobile hadn't struck something. It looked like a man. Everyone gasped and careened forward as Mr. Dimwitty slammed on the brake. His reaction time was pretty good for an old man, but it wasn't good enough. The figure, man or boy or thing, was pinned under the wheels of the car.

Nobody said anything, not even the victim. We were all in a stupor. I don't know how long we sat without stirring, barely breathing, but I was the first to recover.

"Mr. Dimwitty, are you okay? Mr. Dimwitty?" He sat staring through the windshield into the rows of corn. His face, by now, was the color of milk.

"I-I've killed somebody," was his reply. "Some poor farmer. Can you see him? Can anyone see him?"

I admit that I had no wish to look under the car to see who we'd murdered. Still, somebody had to investigate. My hand closed over door handle. I was prepared to face the worst; and then I stopped. Someone was running in our direction.

"What in tarnations is going on here?" To my relief, Dad was standing over us. His face looked black enough to cause rain, but I didn't care. I was happy to see him. He would set things right.

"Why didn't you pull over when I flagged you, Arthur? You were driving too fast."

By now, Mr. Dimwitty had collapsed face down upon his steering wheel and was crying like a baby.

"I've killed someone. Ran right over him. Didn't mean to. Didn't mean to."

"Killed who?" Dad bent down to look under the wheels of the Oldsmobile. A moment later he stood up again and opened the roadster's door on the driver's side.

"Get out of the car, Arthur."

"Y-You going to arrest me?" The old man held out his thin wrists, expecting to be cuffed.

"Just get out of the car. And you boys, too. Is anyone hurt?"

Mr. Dimwitty's eyes widened. "D-Did you hear what I said, John? H-He's under the car."

"I heard you all right. Nothing wrong with *my* hearing."

"W-Well is he... d-dead?"

"Kinda hard to kill a scarecrow, Arthur. Now get out of the car like I said. I want to make sure everyone's okay."

"Scarecrow?" Mr. Dimwitty echoed. "I-Is that all I hit?"

"Well, don't look so happy about it. This is Homer Nordling's field. He'll probably want compensation for his loss. And you're going to get a speeding ticket. A big one."

"A ticket? Yes, yes. I'll pay it. I'll be glad to pay it." The old man danced with glee as if he'd won the Irish Sweepstakes. But a moment later, a new thought sobered him.

"Do you have to tell Alice, John? I mean, we can keep this between ourselves, can't we?"

Alice Gumble was Mr. Dimwitty's middle-aged daughter. Being a widower, he lived with her and her husband Charles.

Charles worked as an assistant in Daniel Maidand's shop and he loved cars. It was an interest the old man shared with his son-in-law but one which was a source of conflict between husband and wife. Alice didn't want her father to drive. She was afraid for him on account of his poor hearing. "Why, he could mow someone down and never hear the screams," she'd been known to complain.

Dad shook his head when he heard the old man's question. "I don't see how we can keep it quiet, Arthur. Homer's got to be told and there's the ticket."

"Maybe Mr. Nordling won't say anything," I piped up, wanting to be of help. The gesture was stupid. Dad's attention turned to me and the rest of the gang who'd formed a half circle of support behind Mr. Dimwitty.

"'You boys are the source of this trouble, aren't you? Wanting him too drive fast?"

"No, no. It wasn't like that," Eric spoke out. "We thought it was an emergency. We were trying to get off the road."

"Well, you certainly managed that didn't you? Lucky none of you was hurt."

"No sir, we're fine," Luscious assured him.

Dad's eyes fell again on Mr. Dimwitty. "I want you to follow me back to the school. No arguments. Alice will be there. You might as well face the music 'cause a thing like this can't be kept quiet."

The old man nodded with a bowed head, knowing that what he'd heard was true.

"Okay. Now you boys get into the Ford. You're riding back with me."

To Dad's surprise, a general whoop went up among the gang. We'd had our fill of the red roadster. Riding in a police car was a stroke of luck we'd never imagined.

"Can we blow the siren, sir?" Derrick gazed up at my dad, his eyes shining with admiration.

"You bet," was the answer.

When we reached Madison, the school cafeteria was full of people milling about. Even Reverend Bolstrand was present, which surprised me. Mom explained that he'd left the parade when he saw Mr. and Mrs. Katafias take off. He thought if there was some emergency, he could help and in a way there was. Turned out, Mrs. Katafias remembered she'd left the oven on after removing some pies for the potluck. She was afraid the house might burn down. Fortunately, it didn't, but by the time she got home, the kitchen was warm enough to bake bread, according to the Reverend. "All's well that ends well," he's reported to have said as he bit into one of Aunt Enid's walnut stuffed cookies.

Those stuffed cookies were a favorite among many who attended the annual Thanksgiving potluck. On those occasions when my aunt could not attend, the disappointment registered by customers at the dessert table always put Mrs. Carlson in a huff, as she prided herself on her pecan pies. She'd been a classmate of my aunt's when they'd attended Madison but, according to my relative, the two of them were never friends.

"Elvira always had a mean and competitive spirit," Aunt Enid had recalled at the dinner table the evening before the 1939 Thanksgiving potluck. Mom frowned, as she objected to gossip, especially when we were eating, but her sister went on anyway.

"I recall once in the third grade, when we were playing jacks at recess and I was ahead -- I was doing pigs in a pen at the time -- she got so mad she picked up all my stars and tossed them into the sandbox."

"She did?" Herman sat wide eyed. Mrs. Carlson was his Sunday school teacher, and he didn't like her much. He complained that she never smiled and lectured in a monotone that put him to sleep.

"She certainly did," Aunt Enid assured him, "and she wasn't very honest, either..."

"Pie anyone?" Mom broke in with a sharp edge to her voice.

"No thank you," replied our aunt, ignoring her younger sister's disapproval. She went on, "I remember one time, we were having a test, geography I think..."

"That would be with Mrs. Wyerick," I groaned.

Aunt Enid's eyes floated toward the ceiling as she considered what I'd said. "You know, I think it was. Nice woman, but honestly, all those pop quizzes..."

I looked up at Mom for a bit of understanding. She seemed to read my thoughts but offered no sympathy. "Mrs. Wyerick is a wonderful teacher."

"I agree Elsie, but the woman was obsessed about geography. Well anyway, we were having this pop quiz which nobody but me and maybe John Griffiths were ready for. You remember him, don't you? That tall kid with the red hair whose father ended up in the Foreign Service somewhere. China, I think it was. Oh, I had such a crush on John. And I think it was mutual because he used to tease me by pulling out the ribbons in my pigtails. I wonder what ever happened to him."

"Didn't you hear?" said Mom as she sliced into a golden crusted apple pie. "He's supposed to have died young. Some illness he caught in China."

Aunt Enid sat back in her chair and stared at her sister. "When did you hear this?"

"Years ago. Reverend Bolstrand kept in touch with the family."

"Oh, I'm so sorry to hear he's gone. Such a smart boy and so full of innocent mischief. Not like Elvira," she added.

"I think you're being too hard on her."

"Oh Elsie, you can't mean that. My word, just look how she lords it over everyone now that she's a doctor's wife. Honestly, she's so full of medical advice you'd think an MD came with her M.R.S."

Both Dad and Uncle Henry let out a guffaw while the third man at the table, Aunt Enid's husband, was wise enough to stuff pie into his mouth.

"What are you two laughing about?" asked Mom as her cheeks turned rosy. "I can't see that Elvira's done either of you any harm."

Dad kept quiet after his rebuke, following Uncle Herschel's example. Uncle Henry, on the other hand, was not one to hold back his thoughts. "Just 'cause a snake hasn't bitten doesn't mean it wouldn't if it could."

"Henry!" Mom's jawed dropped in surprise.

"Oh don't look so shocked, Elsie," said Aunt Enid, coming to her brother's defense. "Henry's like our father. He's got a keen insight and an honest tongue." The older sister leaned a bit further in the rebel's direction. "And just like him, he's got a good sense of humor, too. I wish you'd spend more time with Doggett and me, Henry. I could do with a good laugh now and again, especially after working all day. Besides, there's more for you to do in Columbus." Uncle Henry returned his sister's smile with a crooked one of his own.

"I'd like to, Enid, but then who'd take care of my two nephews?"

"Give 'em a good laugh, you mean?" Aunt Enid winked. Uncle Henry said nothing but threw a side glance at my mom as if he feared he might have offended her.

"Yes, I know," Mom said as she dropped another slice of pie on a plate and set it before her brother. "You two are the ones blessed with a sense of humor. I'm just plain old vanilla, aren't I?"

Aunt Enid's eyebrows rose so high they almost looped behind

her ears. "And what's wrong with vanilla, Elsie? Mama was plain vanilla and who didn't love her? I never got the opportunity to have children, but anyone can see it's a hard job. These boys are lucky. And so's Henry. You take care of him just like Mama did."

Uncle Henry nodded and seeing it, Mom's cheeks went rosy again. "Well, I try to provide a good home..."

"And you do. But that shouldn't prevent Henry from speaking his mind. He's right about Elvira Carlson. She's as cantankerous as they come, always wanting to seem more important than she is. Why I wouldn't be surprised if..."

Mom's hands fanned the air as if they were windshield wipers. "Please, Enid. Have your opinions, if you must, but remember there are children present."

Stopped in mid sentence, Mom's sister sat eyeing Herman and me as if weighing the damage her opinion might do. Finally she reached for a plate and grunted, "Some of that wonderful pie should keep me quiet."

After that, the conversation turned to politics. Herman and I asked to be excused from the table, but I couldn't forget what I'd heard about Mrs. Carlson. The next day at the potluck I kept an eye out for her, curious to see how she would greet my aunt. I remember that I was standing at the dessert table when I first caught a glimpse of her. Her mouse-colored hair was snarled in a bun and the flowered dress she wore, large to accommodate her size, seemed too demure for her steely blue eyes. She was headed in my direction where I stood next to Mr. Dimwitty. His daughter was having conniptions about the scarecrow.

"That's it, Pop. It could have been a person. Don't you see I'm right? You shouldn't be driving."

"Hello, Enid," said Mrs. Carlson, ignoring Alice Gumble's

hullabaloo. Her eyes had a snake-like fix on my aunt, just as Uncle Henry had described it. "I believe it's my time to work. You may consider yourself relieved."

"Why thank you, Elvira." My aunt smiled sweetly. "Relieved is exactly what I am."

Mrs. Carlson gave my aunt a sharp look, not knowing how to take the remark. Her eyes scanned the rows of pies and cakes and cookies. "My, my, look at that. Your stuffed walnuts are almost gone. You really should share your recipe sometime. Heaven knows, I've asked often enough."

"Yes, you have," replied my aunt dismissively as she pulled off her apron. "And heaven knows when you'll get it."

Mrs. Carlson uttered a forced laugh. "You should be more charitable, Enid. I'd be glad to share my pecan pie recipe, if you want."

"That's very kind, Elvira. But I have a recipe of my own."

"Oh yes, but not like mine."

"No, not like yours at all." How Aunt Enid kept from adding the words "It's better," I do not know, because I could see them forming on her lips. She started to walk away, which no doubt was her notion of treating Mrs. Carlson with charity, but the other woman wasn't ready to let go.

"Is your husband with you this year? What is he now... a car salesman?"

Aunt Enid stopped as though she'd been shot in the back. She turned slowly to look her old nemesis in the eye, and anyone could see that the smile on her face was more menacing than friendly. "He owns a Studebaker dealership, Elvira. We drove down from Columbus in the latest model. You might consider a new car yourself. People say that old Hudson your husband drives to make house calls can be heard coughing and chugging all over town."

"People? What people?"

"I didn't make a list, dear. I'm just saying you should come see us sometime. Herschel will be glad to look after you. . . unless, of course, you can't afford a new car."

Mrs. Carlson uttered another forced laugh. "Why, of course we can afford a new car, if we want it. But the Hudson is holding up fine."

"How old is that rattle trap?"

"It's not a 'rattle trap'..."

"A good ten years, at least. You wouldn't want Edgar to get stranded some cold night because of that old car, would you?"

"No, of course not. But as I said..."

Aunt Enid gave her former classmate a gentle pat on the shoulder as she backed away. "Better come see us, Elvira. Herschel will make you an offer you deserve."

Mrs. Carlson stood with her mouth open as my relative moved toward the beverage table. By then, my aunt's smile was genuine and wide enough to drive a Studebaker through.

Safe to say, the days came and went and Mrs. Carlson never did take up her old classmate's offer on the Studebaker. She did get a new car, though. Well, not new exactly, but new to her. About a month after the potluck, she drove home in a 1934 red roadster. Apparently, Alice had worn Mr. Dimwitty down until he agreed to sell his prized possession. Word was that he stayed skulking in the house for days afterwards, refusing to step one foot outside. He said he felt naked without his automobile.

Finally Alice got so worried about her father that she called the doctor, though she was afraid he might drive up to house in the Oldsmobile. He didn't. He came in his Hudson, which was the first car he'd bought after his horse and buggy. He loved that old rattle trap as dearly as Mr. Dimwitty had loved his roadster and after diagnosing the cause of his patient's malaise, he gave the old man a prescription that was strong enough to send him out into the streets in his pajamas. "I'm saved. Thank God Almighty. I'm saved."

True to his word, that very day the doctor had that 1934 red roadster parked in its familiar place in front of the Gumble's house. He hadn't needed another car, no matter what his wife said. Word was he'd been glad to be rid of it. Dad was the one to come home with the story about Mr. Dimwitty getting back his car.

"Blamed fools," he said as he snapped open the evening paper. "People are always wanting what they don't need."

He might have been right in his opinion. He usually was. But I was inclined to think that the difference between 'wanting' and 'needing' wasn't always easy to tell. At such times, Reverend Bolstrand's notion was best: "All's well that ends well."

Chapter 9 - Angel McBride and the Sonja Henie Doll

Photograph: *Oliver and Angel McBride having a snowball fight on the front lawn, December 1939*

Angel McBride knew a thing or two about being independent. That's because her mother, widowed since 1937, had to work long hours as a waitress at the Marabar diner. That left Angel plenty of time to formulate her own views of the world, and they didn't leave much room for grey areas. Some of her sixth grade classmates complained that she was mulish. I thought she was plucky.

Did I forget to mention that Angel was a Catholic? In our town, most of us were Methodists, which might explain why her ideas could seem foreign -- not that anyone held her religion against her. Not me and the guys on my baseball team. For a female, Angel was all right. She didn't cry or make a fuss like other girls when they were teased, and there were lots of remarks about her masses of curly red hair. She made a pretty fair first baseman, too, if the team was short a player. But the truth was, outside of class, she tended to keep to herself. I suppose it was because Mrs. McBride depended upon Angel to look after things at home.

Most people saw no problem with the arrangement between mother and daughter -- none that is, except Mrs. Carlson, who had the temerity to voice her opinion one slow day when I was sitting with my dad at the Marabar. If Angel became a Methodist she crowed, loud enough to be heard clear across the

125

railroad tracks a quarter of a mile away, then "the child wouldn't be left so much on her own and besides, a dollop of Bible studies wouldn't do her character no harm."

Mrs. McBride, pouring coffee into my dad's cup, froze behind the counter, as did everyone else seated on their stools. If she was known for one thing besides her blaze of red hair, it was for her lethal rejoinders. She could drop a truck driver at fifty paces if she'd a mind to, so Mrs. Carlson, church elder or not, was a fool to invite a retort. But Mrs. Carlson, twenty years older and holding a 60 pound advantage over her opponent, apparently didn't think so.

Angel's mother continued to stand with her mouth agape, letting the coffee spill over my dad's cup. If he hadn't wrestled the pot from her hands, the whole counter would have been awash. That done, he turned an avenging eye on Mrs. Carlson.

"Angel McBride doesn't need to become a Methodist. Anyone with eyes can see the church in her heart!" Dad winked at those closest to him, a signal that he doubted the same could be said of Mrs. Carlson. The gesture provoked more than a few smiles and caused the church elder to swing on her heels and stomp out the door.

Had I been called to testify, I would have agreed with Dad's assessment of the youngest McBride. Angel had a fierce belief in her Maker. Take, for example, the summer Bodacious Scurvy went missing. A general rejoicing was heard at the Marabar because Bodacious had tangled with many a hostile member of our community, and they bore the scars to prove it. Angel was not among these. She liked the alley cat, held his independence in high regard and announced she was going to pray for his deliverance.

"Don't waste your breath on that flea-bitten animal," I objected. "God's not interested in the comings and goings of no alley cat."

Angel planted her hands on her hips and glared at me. "He made Bodacious, didn't he?" I nodded. "Then that proves He cares."

Fortunately, I was not foolish enough to bet Angel that she was wrong and I'm glad because not more than three days passed before a second whoop went up at the diner. A few pounds lighter, his hair matted and with eyes that exhibited a peculiar glaze, Bodacious Scurvy alighted from the rear of a parked truck, took a moment to orient himself, then swaggered into the shade of a nearby sycamore, tail up and shoulders squared. Angel was quick to make a fuss over him, arriving with some scraps her mom supplied. These he took from her as if it were his due.

Asked about the cat, the truck driver looked surprised. He swiveled round on his stool as though he'd been told he'd forgotten to set his brake. Spying Bodacious stretched out in the shade, he let out a chuckle.

"Oh him! Found him this morning under some tarps. Don't know where he's from."

"Here," said a voice at the end of the counter. "Must have joined up with you on your last run. How long's that been?"

"Six days round trip," the driver replied.

Mrs. McBride, who was setting more scraps aside for the cat's supper, asked the question on everyone's mind. "Wonder how Bodacious lasted in all this heat?"

The driver chuckled a second time. "Pshaw! No mystery to that! Not if you know what I was hauling." He tossed a few coins on the counter then headed toward the door with a dozen pair of eyes at his back.

Oscar, the proprietor, came out of the kitchen, curious enough to leave his bacon sizzling. "Well, what was it? What were you hauling?"

The man in the red bandanna tossed us a grin over his shoulder. "Whiskey! A crate of it broke. Don't 'xpect that cat of yours'll be happy with water ever again!" He made his exit amidst the roar of loud guffaws.

I was having a pretty good time myself, till Angel sidled up to me and whispered. "What did I tell you, Oliver? God moves in mysterious ways."

After the hubbub about Bodacious Scurvy died down, the story of his return having been told and retold with embellishments, the rest of the summer passed sleepily as most summers did. I gave no further thought to God's mysterious ways until the trees had lost their leaves. And it was close to Christmas.

Snow was falling the day I found Angel outside the hardware store, her nose pressed against the glass as if it were frozen to the spot. I stopped to inquire about her fascination and that's when she pointed to a shelf crammed with dolls behind Mr. Swanson's cash register. Most of them were bride dolls, dressed in white with satin ribbons and veils but one stood out among the rest: a Sonja Henie doll wearing a red velvet tunic that was trimmed in rabbit fur and a pair of silver ice skates. All in all, it cut a pretty fair replica of the Olympic ice skating champion.

"You gonna ask Santa for it?" I sniggered and gave her a jab in the ribs.

"I'm gonna do better than that," she replied, returning my jab. "I'm gonna pray."

When I heard that my eyelids snapped up like a pair of broken blinds. "Criminally, Angel, you can't ask God for no doll! That's blasphemy or somethin'. Why don't you ask your mother, instead? Leastwise it would be more practical."

128

The look I received for my suggestion could have burned toast. "My mom can't afford to buy no dolls, Larson. Do you know how much they cost?"

I shook my head to say that I didn't.

"Well I'll tell you. A week's wages. That's what it would cost. Do you think I'd ask my mom for a doll when she hasn't had a new winter coat in six years?"

I shook my head again.

"That's right I wouldn't!" Angel gave the Sonja Henie doll a second glance. "Nope. If I'm to have that doll, it's up to God!"

Unlike most kids, the closer it came to Christmas, the more depressed I got. Partly it was because I missed Albert, the hobo, and partly because I was tapped for the school's Christmas pageant, an event I dreaded, and partly because I was pretty sure there'd be no Sonja Henie doll under Angel's tree. Mr. Swanson told me how much it cost -- too much for me to afford with only a paper route. The best I could do was send up a couple of prayers on Angel's behalf, too. Given my record, though, I wasn't expecting any miracles.

To my surprise, a few days before Christmas the Sonja Henie doll disappeared. I rushed into the Hardware store full of hope. Maybe our prayers, Angel's and mine, had been answered. Maybe Mrs. McBride had gotten a bonus or something and she'd bought the doll for Angel. Or maybe Mr. Swanson... No. Mr. Swanson counted his pennies. It had to be Mrs. McBride who'd bought the doll! When I asked, the proprietor laughed.

"Why are you so interested in that doll, Ollie? Were ya hoping to get one for Christmas?"

I didn't laugh, so the old man scratched his snowy head and looked serious. He smiled after a time. "Yah sure, it was that carpet salesman on his way to Columbus. He was worried about the on-coming storm. Didn't haggle. Paid full price and had me wrap it for his daughter who was down with the croup. Said his girl loved Sonja Henie. Bought some tire chains, too."

If I'd have been a good Christian, I should have been happy for the child in Columbus, but instead I resented her. She was going to get the ribboned box that should have gone to my friend. It wasn't fair. My cheeks must have burned because Mrs. Swanson asked me if l were coming down with something. I said no and walked out of the shop in disgust.

The dime store was a few paces ahead of me. I went in with the last 25 cents of my pocket money and bought Angel a bottle of "Evening in Paris," mainly because that's what it cost and because Ione Hjalmer, who worked behind the counter and who had just turned eighteen, said the name conjured up the mystery of far away places. Anyway, I liked the blue bottle with its silver label.

On Christmas Eve, I ran into Angel at her post, staring through the window of Mr. Swanson's hardware store. A lump formed in my throat as I walked up to her, wondering what I was going to say.

"It's gone, Larson. The doll's gone." The green eyes turned in my direction showed no sign of tears.

Angel was tougher than I thought, but I still felt sad for her. "G-Gee, t-that's too bad," I stuttered, "Somebody must of bought it. M-Maybe one of those traveling salesmen on his way to Columbus."

If I'd had let bees nest in my hair, Angel couldn't have looked more surprised. "Oh, ye of little faith, Larson! If you can't figure out what's happened to it, you'll just have to wait till Christmas." She smiled and then left me with a jaunty walk, as if she hadn't a care in the world.

My shoulders slumped. Angel McBride thought she was going to get the Sonja Henie doll for Christmas and she was headed for a fall. The little blue bottle stashed in my jacket could do nothing to save her.

Christmas morning dawned with a fresh dusting of snow. Herman was up before the birds, but I stayed in bed long enough for Mom to wonder if I might need a dose of cod liver oil. By the time I shambled into the living room, my limbs feeling like cold spaghetti, Herman had fingered every present under the tree. He shoved a red and green package into my gut, furious that I'd been slow to rise as it was a family rule that no gifts were opened until everyone was assembled. I wanted to crown him, but I didn't. This year, I hoped Christmas would be different, less about presents and more about good feelings.

The box Herman had so rudely delivered contained a pair of gloves exactly like the ones I'd circled in the Sears catalogue. Apparently, Uncle Henry had seen my mark because he beamed like a jack-o-lantern when I whooped with delight. Even though I was twelve, I gave him a hug to show him he was special. But it wasn't for the gloves only. Uncle Henry was one person who kept Christmas in his heart all year round.

After breakfast, I put on my coat and cap to head for Angel's house. I had to know how she was doing. Dad looked surprised as usually Herman and I spent the better part of Christmas morning wrangling over which one of us got the best presents. I told my folks where I was headed and Dad gave Mom a wink like he thought I might be sweet on Angel. I didn't explain but hurried out the door where the temperature was as cold as a truant officer's heart. Even with my new gloves, I had to drive my hands into my jacket pockets. That's when I discovered the bottle of Evening in Paris. It'd had been there since I bought it. It wasn't wrapped and seemed so small in my hand.

Angel's house was just a few doors down from mine, but I

walked so slowly that it seemed like a mile. I could see the smoke rising from the McBride's chimney, but other than that the house was still. Angel's mother, I knew, would be at work. Oscar never closed the Marabar and as he was a Jew, he had no fondness for Christmas. Rapping softly at the red door, I hoped that Mrs. McBride, because of the holiday, had taken her daughter with her. But a second later, a bolt snapped free and Angel stood in the door way, her eyelids red as pomegranates from crying.

The minute she saw me, she flung her arms around my neck. She didn't say a word. She didn't have to. I hugged her back, not caring what the neighbors might think or if Paddy O'Malley and the entire baseball team walked by. Angel's heart was broken and my job was to hold her together.

When her whimpers subsided, I handed her the bottle of Evening in Paris. I wasn't thinking of it as a gift, more like a distraction. Angel took it from me with her slim fingers and held it toward the sky. Against the light, the glass burst into a multitude of shades, azure, turquoise, sapphire, so that it was framed in a delicate aura. Even I could barely take my eyes away, although I did notice that Angel's expression had changed. It was filled with wonder as if she were seeing all those far away places that Ione had talked about. That's when I began to think there might be some magic in that little blue bottle. Maybe it was a sign that Angel should leave her thoughts of dolls behind and look to the future. Anyway, she was happy and so was I.

We didn't talk about God and prayer after that. I don't mean that Angel lost her faith. She didn't. And when she took her first Holy Communion I was there, struck by how beautiful she looked in her white gown and veil.

To be honest, I don't know how she reconciled her disappointment about the doll, nor did I give much thought to the incident until years later. I'd been away from home a long time only to return for a brief visit. By then, I knew that Angel had married a carpenter named Erickson who loved her enough to become a Catholic. I could understand why.

We met by accident on Main Street. Angel was pushing a pram, beaming as new mothers do. The little girl was beautiful, just as I would have expected.

"What's she called?" I said straightening up from the pram to look my friend in the eye.

"Patricia, after my mom."

"Patricia?"

"Yeah. Don't you like the name, Larson?"

"No, no. Patricia's a lovely name. I just thought it might be... well... Sonja."

"Sonja?" Angel blinked as if I'd been foolish enough to wear ribbons in my hair. "Why ever..." Then a light dawned. A memory burst into flames and I saw again that confident smile.

"What have I always told you, Larson? God moves in mysterious ways."

Chapter 10 - The Stick That Melted

Photograph: *Henry in his tap dancing shoes with Recalcitrant,*
February 1940

Uncle Henry came to visit us in 1936 and stayed, claiming he'd had a premonition that if he left town something terrible would happen. My father, who was usually skeptical about premonitions, took Uncle Henry's side in this. Moving, he told my mother sarcastically, would mean the end of free meals and the possibility that Uncle Henry would have to get a job.

Mother always frowned at the charge. Her brother, younger by two years, wasn't lazy, she insisted. He suffered from an "artistic soul." My father would howl like a man who'd had an iron dropped on his foot when he'd hear this, but seldom in my mother's presence.

Still, my mom's position was vindicated by a small manila envelope that arrived in the mail one day in mid-winter. "Congratulations!" the letter began. Apparently, Uncle Henry had won one of the bazillion jingle contests he was always entering.

"There! You see!" My mother flapped the letter in front of my dad's face as he crossed the threshold that evening. "It says here Henry's won a prize. I told you he was artistic."

Dad grunted as he pulled off his boots, unwilling to return my mother's gaze. "What's for supper?" was all he said and then he tried to push past her into the living room. Mom stood her ground and waved the letter in his face a second time. "He

135

wrote the winning jingle. It says so! Here!"

If there was to be any peace, Dad had to give in. He took the paper from her, holding it as if it were a used hanky, and let his eyes drift down the page. When he let out a snort, it took everyone by surprise. "Says here your brother's won himself a pair of tap dancing shoes, Elsie. Now isn't that wonderful? Especially since there's no dance studio here. 'Course, he could move in with your sister, Enid, over in Columbus. They've got teachers there. Heck, I'd be glad to buy him a one-way bus ticket."

Dad may have savored the moment of his sarcasm, but it was short lived. Mom had her ways of getting back at him and she wasn't subtle. When the family sat down to supper that night, we were given cold cuts instead of the stew that had been simmering on the stove all afternoon.

The story didn't end there, either. A week later those shoes arrived and Uncle Henry discovered that he'd been sent a pair of lady's slippers, size thirteen, complete with two-inch heels and ribbons that tied into bows. They were too large for Mom, so Uncle Henry took to wearing them. He imagined he'd have bad luck if he looked a gift horse in the mouth.

At first, he tottered around the house, stiff-legged and uncomfortable; but in time the shoes stretched and he got the hang of walking on the balls of his feet. He delighted in the clickety-clack sound they made and that gave him the idea to go outside and try them on the pavement. When the neighbors saw him they refused to believe their eyes and in a small town like ours, everyone had an opinion about Uncle Henry and his tap dancing shoes.

"People think he's crazy, Elsie!" Dad blustered one morning while Uncle Henry was out for his dance shoe constitutional.

Mom stood at the counter at the time, rolling out biscuit dough.

Why should they think that? What's crazy about a man out for a walk?"

"Those shoes, Elsie. Those shoes!"

"What's wrong with those shoes?"

"THEY HAVE RIBBONS ON THEM!"

"So?"

"Don't you think it's a little strange for a man to be wearing tap dancing shoes with high heels and ribbons on them?"

"As if you've never worn ribbons!"

Her tone was so certain, so accusatory that Dad was taken aback. "What? I've never worn ribbons in my life!"

"What about your army jacket? When you were in the service?"

"Those aren't ribbons, Elsie, and you know it. Those are medals."

"You call them ribbons."

"Yes, but they're medals."

"They look like ribbons."

"Elsie, are you trying to give me an ulcer?"

Dad retreated to the living room, afraid that if he persisted, there'd be cold cuts for breakfast. But his face was a blue-green portrait of exasperation. He could think of no way to make his wife see reason when it came to her brother. Still, if he had known what was going to happen next, he might have reconciled himself to the status quo. But he couldn't foresee the future, or the day when his patience would be sorely tested: the day Uncle Henry came home with a lost dog!

The German shepherd had followed him home, my relative said -- mesmerized no doubt by the sound of those tapping shoes -- and he had named it Recalcitrant. Why Uncle Henry had chosen that moniker no one understood because the dog had impeccable manners and even knew some tricks, as we soon discovered. Nonetheless, Recalcitrant was what we called him and, being a smart dog, he soon answered to the name.

When Herman and I came home from elementary school that first day and saw the tan and black police dog dozing on our kitchen floor, we were delighted and amazed. Dad had always been adamant about his "no pets" rule, but Mom liked Recalcitrant and we half hoped that we could keep him. We hung around the kitchen until the hall clock struck five, the time Dad usually came home, so we could see the look on his face as he came through the door. Uncle Henry was out at the time, but Mom went on peeling potatoes at the sink as if having a dog in our kitchen was as natural as sunshine.

When he found us, Dad was waving his newspaper in the air, complaining about those rascals in Washington D.C. who always wanted to solve problems by throwing money at it. Why, if he were in the Congress...

With both his feet planted in the room it wasn't long before he caught sight of the dog lying by the stove. He didn't say anything at first, but his jaw dropped and he blinked like one of those neon signs we'd seen in Columbus the previous summer. Herman and I knew what that look meant and snapped to attention. Of course, Recalcitrant didn't know any better. He wagged his tail like he was expecting a pat on the head. When that didn't happen, he roused himself and padded across the room to sit at the stranger's feet.

By now the skin on Dad's neck was a beet red. My brother and

I knew he could blow at any minute if someone didn't explain why a German Shepherd was drooling on his shoes! Unfortunately, Mom had decided to meet Dad's silence with a silence of her own. She stood with her back to him, tossing the diced potatoes into a pot of boiling water. The tension in the air was thick enough to dice as well. Herman couldn't take it. He started to wheeze and that's when Dad cut loose.

"Oliver, you know better than to bring a dog into the house. Just listen to your brother! Take this animal back to where you found it. Right now, ya hear?"

"But it's not mine..." I started to explain that the dog belonged to Uncle Henry but Dad wasn't listening.

"Or take it to the Humane Society if it doesn't have a home. Just get rid of it."

Recalcitrant didn't much care for Dad's tone. He growled and bared his teeth, behavior which would have given pause to an ordinary man. But Dad, who'd been awarded a medal for bravery, was no ordinary man. He grabbed the dog by its collar with one hand and with the other he gave me a shake. Herman and I howled, which brought Recalcitrant to our defense, barking and snapping in earnest. That's when Mom stepped in.

"Stop it, John. Let go of that dog. And let go of Oliver, too! Henry brought the animal home. Poor thing's lost so I said we'd keep him until we found the owner. Anyone can see this is no stray. Someone's given Recalcitrant lots of care."

"Recalcitrant?"

"That's his name. At least that's what Henry calls him. So, we will, too, until we find out who owns him."

"That's the stupidest name for a dog I ever heard."

"Be that as it may, it's his for the time being."

"But what about Herman's allergy?"

"I guess he's grown out of it. He's been petting the animal all afternoon. He didn't start wheezing until you came home and made a scene."

"So it's my fault, is it?"

"It's nobody's fault, John. I know you mean well, but the dog isn't doing any harm. And Henry promises to take care of it. You don't have to do a thing."

"No? Just pay for an extra mouth to feed."

Supper that evening was quiet, mainly because Dad sat drafting an ad about the dog for the "Lost and Found" column of the local paper. Recalcitrant's days with us were numbered and the rest of the family felt sad.

Come the next morning, Recalcitrant was behaving meek as a lamb. Dad was the one barking. "That animal is Uncle Henry's responsibility," he said at the breakfast table. He shook a finger at Herman and me for emphasis. "I don't want either of you walking that dog, or playing with that dog or petting that dog. You hear?"

My brother and I sat wide-eyed and silent. Uncle Henry, in his mocking tone, answered for us. "That's right! You boys listen to your father. Recalcitrant's my dog. Don't either of you go breaking the law in this house and having a bit of fun."

Dad threw his napkin on the table when he heard that and ordered me to follow him into the hallway. "Blamed fool," he muttered. "Half the time he doesn't know what's going on!"

If it had been my place to contradict, I'd have said that Uncle

Henry knew what was going on more than most people realized. His goofiness and pretending not to understand was a way of getting back at anyone who annoyed him. But, as I say, it wasn't for me to comment.

Dad bent down and placed a quarter in my hand. "Get some scraps from the butcher's before you head for school, Oliver. That uncle of yours doesn't know how to care for an animal. He's just as likely to feed it popcorn."

I was so surprised by my dad's concern for the dog that I stood in the open door watching him head for the precinct, his coin still warm in my hand.

About that time, Uncle Henry decided to take Recalcitrant for a walk. He put on his dancing shoes, as usual, and I followed him out the door on my father's errand. The neighbors' drapes fluttered as he clicked by on the snow-shoveled sidewalk and when he guessed the audience was large enough, he stopped and danced a little jig. Recalcitrant liked the game and danced too, or at least leaped into the air and barked so that the pair made quite a commotion. There must have been some tsk, tsk, tsking from behind those curtains, but I'll bet the righteous were unprepared for the finale. His dance done, Uncle Henry reached into the snow and hurled snowballs at a few windows so that the panes wobbled like jelly. Then he bowed to an invisible audience and sauntered down the street with his dog at his heels.

On my way back from the butcher's, I spied Uncle Henry in the park, standing in the center of the tennis court. Despite the snow, the net was in place and my relative was trying to teach Recalcitrant to leap over it, like a horse in a steeple chase. At first the animal didn't understand and kept running around the poles, end to end, in a one dog race. But when he saw Uncle Henry take a sudden leap, he got the idea. Uncle Henry leaped again and this time, the dog followed. They must have thought it was a marvelous game, because I left them there, hopping from one side of the net to the other on that snow covered tennis court.

This net practice went on for two days, and even Mom noticed how eager man and dog were to be off to the park. She told Dad that she'd never seen Uncle Henry so happy. Having a pet to care for seemed to give him a purpose. And there was no doubt the dog loved Uncle Henry.

"Now, Elsie," my father warned, guessing where the conversation was headed. "As you said, Recalcitrant is somebody's pet. He can't stay with us forever."

Dad must have been clairvoyant because a day later, Recalcitrant's owners showed up at our door. Uncle Henry and the dog were at the park at the time. The couple said they had seen our notice in the paper and that Recalcitrant's real name was Boniface-Ignacio-Don Ducchio III or some such foolishness as people assign to pedigrees. He was a performance dog and the winner of several awards. They'd lost Boniface at a gas station on their way to a dog show in Akron and had been combing the area looking for him.

From their pinched expressions I could see that they were worried, but that didn't incline me to like them. Apparently, Herman felt the same way because he kept insisting that the dog we'd found was a Labrador. Finally, my mom told him to hush and said that Mr. and Mrs. Bryant could wait in the living room until her brother came home. Mom tried to put on a good face, but I could see in her eyes that she wasn't any happier than Herman or I.

While we waited, Mom made small talk with our visitors. My brother and I sat at a distance, glaring at the strangers as if they were thieves. Finally, Mr. Bryant grew uncomfortable enough to reach into his wallet and offer us a reward. Herman held out his hand, but Mom slapped it back and said that finding the dog's owners was reward enough.

After that, there was a lull in the conversation until the kettle whistled and Mom went into the kitchen to make tea. My brother and I stayed behind, in case Mr. Bryant decided to renew his offer of a reward, which he didn't.

An uncomfortable silence fell until Mom came back with a plate of oatmeal cookies. These she offered to the Bryants and then to Herman and me. Naturally, my brother and I reached for the biggest one and were about to have an argument when we heard the clatter of Uncle Henry's tap dancing shoes on the porch steps.. Both of us froze, our hands suspended above the cookie, wondering if we should sound an alarm. "Run, Uncle Henry! Run!"

But it was too late for that. Uncle Henry bounced into the living room before either of us could utter a word. He must have smelled food. He gawked at the strangers in surprise and might have gone out again except that when Recalcitrant saw the pair, he rushed headlong into their outstretched arms.

Mom saw how happy they all were and reached into her apron pocket for a hanky to wipe away her tears. Herman and I didn't know what to think. We sat with our mouths hanging open, mirroring Uncle Henry's expression.

After the reunion, Mr. Bryant shook my uncle's hand and offered a reward a second time. Uncle Henry refused, but I noticed that while they were talking, he was careful to avoid the man's eyes. I guessed he couldn't bear to see the happiness there. Of course, Recalcitrant didn't understand what was about to happen. He sat wagging his tail as if we had become one big, happy family.

Soon after, the Bryants headed for their Oldsmobile and held the rear door open, waiting for Recalcitrant to jump in. The dog didn't move at first. He sat on the sidewalk looking up at Uncle

Henry as if to ask if he was coming, too. When my relative didn't move, the dog seemed to understand.

Lying on the ground nearby was an icicle that had broken from the roof. Recalcitrant picked it up between his teeth and laid it at Uncle Henry's feet, just as he'd done so many times with sticks in the park. "Good boy," said my uncle, reaching down to give the dog a scratch behind the ear. Then he led his companion to the Oldsmobile and watched him jump into the back seat. Recalcitrant barked once and then the car sped away.

For a long time, Uncle Henry stood in the doorway, waving into the vacant street. Mom hadn't the heart to tell him to shut the door as he was letting in the cold air. Eventually he went upstairs, carrying the icicle with him. He took off his dancing shoes and he never wore them again. No one asked why. We didn't have to. The day the stick melted was the only day I ever saw my uncle cry.

Chapter 11 - The Hideout

Photograph: *Oliver standing with Mrs. Hjalmer holding a bowl*
of blackberries, August 1940

I wouldn't call it a hideout, exactly. The place was only habitable during the warm months of the year; but if I wanted to get away from my little brother or escape an errand to the butcher's, or if I wanted to woolgather without being teased by Stubby Norville and the rest of the gang, the blackberry bushes that covered the vacant lot next to the Katafias' house was the place I'd go.

The vines were tall enough for a grown man to stand in without being seen and vigorous enough to claim almost the entire lot. Mrs. Katafias was always waging a war against them from her side of the fence, afraid her tomato plants would be strangled. But, like so much in life, some good came along with the bad. Mom loved those vines. They provided her with enough canned berries and preserves to take the family through the long winter months. "A taste of summer in December," she liked to say as she stood watch over the canning jars that bubbled in their bath, sometimes using her hand to brush away a lock of blonde hair that had been pried loose by the steam.

Of course, I liked blackberries as much of the next person, but as I said, my admiration for them stemmed from the privacy they afforded me. Hiding among the brambles might seem a foolish thing to do on account of the thorns. But if a person had thick gloves and initiative, he could burrow out a space that was not only secret, it was thick enough to blot out the sun on a hot

145

day or provide shelter from the rain... not to mention the seasonal snack one enjoyed while ruminating.

Many of my brilliant schemes came to me while I idled away time in my burrow. Not all of them were good... that is to say, the ideas were good, but some of them I came to regret.

Take for example the occasion of the engagement between Ione Hjalmer to Kermit Dietrick. Kermit was in his early twenties and making his way up the management ladder as a teller in the bank where my father had once cornered a robber. Ione had just graduated from high school and worked at the local five and dime. I liked her well enough, so I don't know why I ruined her wedding shower. I think it was her mother, Mrs. Hjalmer, who put the mischief in me.

The Hjalmer's, like the rest of us, were people of modest means. Mr. Hjalmer was a sawyer. He made his living driving his rusty truck through the neighborhoods, looking for people to pay him to transform their cordwood into fire logs with his circular saw. But the prospect of having a banker in the family seemed to have given Mrs. Hjalmer the notion that she could put on airs.

"I don't think Ione should settle for ordinary dishware," said Mrs. Hjalmer one August afternoon. She was seated at our kitchen table, staring at the chipped mug into which Mom had poured coffee. "She could get a discount where she works; but being a banker's wife, well, Ione's bound to do a bit of entertaining." Our neighbor dumped a teaspoon of sugar into the mug and stirred with her pinky extended.

"A set of china. That's what she needs. Something from the Sears catalogue or maybe from one of those big stores in Columbus. Of course there's always Lennox. Oh wouldn't that be lovely, Elsie? Don't you just love the Lennox china with the gold rim?" Her bird-like eyes shone with the question.

Mom was standing at the stove with her back to our guest, easing a second tray of jam jars into a kettle of boiling water. "Well, I don't know, Dulce. With two boys in the house, I'd want plastic, if I had my druthers."

"Plastic!" Mrs. Hjalmer looked crestfallen. "You mean like those cups and saucers they put in dish washing powder as a promotion? You can't give a bride something like that."

"I didn't realize we were talking about gifts, Dulce. No, I expect one couldn't. But I'd like a set of plastic all the same. Everything I own is chipped. And I don't hold out much hope for that Lennox you're imagining, once Ione starts a family."

"Maybe so, but for a bride... "

Mom turned round to face her guest, crossing her arms as she looked down at the woman whose hair was the color of sandpaper. "Dulce, I know you're anxious about this shower you're giving next month. Naturally, you want everything to be perfect, but Ione is a sensible girl. She knows times are hard. Don't go putting notions of Lennox into her head. I've heard the other ladies talking and she's going to get some nice gifts. Everyone likes Ione."

"I know, I know," said Mrs. Hjalmer, her eyes downcast, as if surveying the spot where she'd spilled sugar on the table. "Ione is a good girl... "

"You raised her right, Dulce. You can be proud of her."

"I am Elsie. I am. That's why I want her life to be better'n mine. She deserves more. You know how it is. We all want more for our kids, especially after the hard times we've all been going through. A little splurge, that's what I want for her."

"Well, I'd say she's got something special already. Kermit's almost too nice for the world of banking."

147

"Yes, he is a good person. But he's lucky, too. As you say, everyone thinks the world of Ione."

"They do. And if she raises youngsters half as good as yours or mine..." Mom paused to ruffle the hair on my head, "Then her life will be blessed."

"I like Ione a lot," I said, feeling that I needed to add to the conversation. "She's been a big help to me with my geography lessons."

"Yes," replied Mrs. Hjalmer thoughtfully. "She was always good at that."

Mom offered Mrs. Hjalmer a freshly baked cookie.

"With all the baking you do, Elsie, I don't know how you stay so slim. I suppose boys are harder on a mother than girls. I'm glad I have Ione. I don't think I'd care to raise boys."

Mom sat down at the table beside Mrs. Hjalmer and raised her mug to her lips but not before saying, sweetly but firmly, "I wouldn't trade mine for the world."

After Mrs. Hjalmer left I asked Mom why our neighbor, who always did seem to look on the bleak side of things, seemed to be a bit moodier than usual.

"Wedding nerves," Mom answered. "That and maybe a little sadness at the thought of losing Ione."

"Losing her? She's moving two blocks down the street for crumb sakes."

"Yes, but Ione won't be just a daughter anymore. She'll be a wife and before we know it, probably a mother."

"Well, Mrs. Hjalmer wouldn't want her to grow into an old

maid, would she?"

"No, she wouldn't. But that doesn't change how she feels about losing a daughter. It's kind of complicated, Oliver."

"Will you feel sad if I get married?"

"Of course not. I'll be happy for you as I can be. But that doesn't mean I won't miss the little boy who tracks mud into the house on rainy days." Mom gave me a hug that was bone crushing, then told me to fetch the Sears catalogue from the living room.

"Whatcha want that for?" I asked, hoping she'd noticed the picture of the catcher's mitt I'd circled on page 569.

"Some of those Lennox pieces are on sale. I think I saw a pretty bud vase that was fifty percent off. Maybe I can surprise Dulce as much as Ione."

After my conversation with Mom and the kindly example she set with regard to Mrs. Hjalmer, I should have been able to follow her example, but I didn't. On the day of the wedding shower, the fates seemed aligned against me. I might have behaved better if there'd been a ball game at the park, or if I hadn't needed to get away from Herman who was nagging me to help him build a fire station with his tinker toys, or if a new Captain Marvel comic book had arrived at the drug store. Then I wouldn't have found myself sitting amongst the blackberries with a clear view of the Hjalmer's front door.

What I observed from my vantage point seemed more like a hijacking than a party. Ione's mother greeted her guests on the front porch. There she relieved them of their gifts -- even shook the packages as if assessing their value -- before allowing anyone into the house. Robin Hood couldn't have done it better, except he would have smiled more. Mrs. Hjalmer was in deadly earnest.

Eventually the line of visitors thinned to a trickle. In my mind's eye, I imagined what was going on inside the house. Mrs. Hjalmer would be hovering near the presents, counting them, caressing them until enough time had lapsed for Ione to begin tearing away the wrappings. Heaven help anyone foolish enough to have brought dish towels or a cutting board. Mrs. Hjalmer had made it clear to my mother and probably everyone else, that she wanted china, gilt-edged china.

The fact that I needed a new catcher's mitt more than Ione needed a stupid vase would never occur to her and probably wouldn't have mattered, believing as she did that Ione should be given the stars if she wanted them. Well, as Mom said, "Pride goeth before a fall"; so when an idea came to me that would teach Mrs. Hjalmer a lesson, I didn't pause to consider the consequences.

I bolted for home as if I'd found a quarter and could hear the jingle of the Good Humor Man's ice cream cart. Herman was sprawled on the living room carpet when I arrived. His tinker toys lay in disarray around him, almost as if he had tossed them into the air to see where they might fall. He glanced up expectantly when I slammed the front door. I saw the pleading look in his eyes but I sprinted past him up the stairs.

"Not now, Herman. Maybe later."

I was headed for a shoe box that was tucked away in our bedroom closet. That's where I kept a few treasures: my Captain Marvel decoder ring and an almost complete set of Play Ball cards with pictures of Joe DiMaggio and Ted Williams among them. In the heat of the moment, I tossed the contents on to the floor, hoping to find a new box for them later.

After that, I scavenged a few minutes in Mom's sewing room and the utility closet, before tiptoeing down the stairs. It wouldn't do for my kid brother to see me carting away a shoebox, tissue paper, ribbons, scissors and a shovel. He'd be bound to ask questions and want to come along. Fortunately, he was sitting with his back to the hallway, trying to jamb pieces of his toy set together without much success. I ran past him faster than a wind could carry me and headed for my hideout.

At the back of the lot was a large ant hill, maybe two feet tall. I'd discovered it a few days earlier and, as the afternoon of the wedding shower was warm and the berries were bursting with juice, I found the area teaming with insect traffic. One scoop with my shovel and I'd collected about a zillion ants and a couple of worms. These I unceremoniously dumped into the empty shoe box and slammed down the lid, securing my prisoners under layers of tissue paper and ribbon. When I'd finished, no one, except a master criminal or maybe a spy, would suspect the innocent looking parcel I held in my hands.

I deposited the package at the Hjalmer's door, rapped twice, loud enough to be heard, then leapt across porch steps and hightailed it for home. For the rest of the afternoon Herman was going to get all the help he needed to build his fire station and I was going to get an alibi.

At dinner that evening, Mom talked of nothing else but the shower. Her pale complexion sported a rosy glow as if she'd emptied her rouge pot on her cheeks and forehead. Rarely had I seen her so upset.

"I tell you John, it was nothing less than an invasion. The ants scurried everywhere, mostly because Ione threw up her hands and let out a screech when she saw what was in the box. Ants and dirt flew through the air. Some of the mess landed on the cake and in the punch.

People scrambled to get out of the way, of course, and that's how the bud vase ended up in pieces."

Dad looked up from his pork chop. "You mean the one you got her? That expensive one?"

"Now don't go on about the cost again. It was on sale. A girl only gets married once and we can afford it, what with you having a steady job."

"Yeah, who said crime doesn't pay?" Uncle Henry snorted.

"That's not funny," Mom scolded. "Nor is leaving a box of ants on a porch disguised as a present. I sure wish I knew who did it. I'd give him such a tongue-lashing."

"What makes you think it's a 'he'?" Dad asked matter-of-factly. Maybe some woman who didn't get invited to the party left it."

"Don't be silly. A woman wouldn't do a thing like that."

"But a grown man would? Is that what you think?"

Mom looked taken aback. "Well no. I suspect some kid was playing a joke." Mom set a bowl of buttered corn ears on the table then turned and glared at me with a hand on one hip.

"I don't suppose you know anything about this do you, Oliver?"

"Me?" I could feel the color rising to my cheeks. "Why do you think it was me?"

"I didn't say it was you. Of course it wasn't you." Mom sounded exasperated. "Your father and I aren't raising hooligans. Besides, you'd have no call to hurt Ione. She's been good to you. No, I meant one of the other boys may have said something, boasted about it."

"N-no," I answered truthfully. "I haven't heard anything. Honest."

Uncle Henry put down his corn cob and stared at me. Maybe I'd been too quick with my disclaimer or my voice sounded too high. Anyway, I could see a question forming in his eyes so I looked away. "Is there any more gravy?"

Mom shoved the tureen in my direction, but Herman intercepted it and emptied most of the contents onto his mashed potatoes. That night I didn't complain.

"And poor Dulce," Mom went on not noticing the greed of her youngest son. "Where she saw the Lennox was smashed, she got down on her hands and knees and tried to salvage the pieces. It wouldn't do her any good, I told her. They weren't big enough to glue together. That's when she broke down and cried. I'd been the only one to bring china, you see. Well, I felt so sorry for her I got down on my knees too and helped pick up the pieces anyway. I wish we could afford another vase, but I know we can't."

"That's right," said Dad as if he were slamming a door.

153

"Herman's got the dentist and there's the life insurance..."

"Oh don't go on, John. I wasn't suggesting we send off for another. But it's a crying shame. Ione's her only child and..."

"How come?" Herman piped up as he stirred gravy into his potatoes.

"What?"

"How come she only has Ione? Why didn't she have another kid?"

"W-Why?" Mom sank into her chair like she might be having a dizzy spell. "I don't think that's a question for a young boy to ask. It's none of your business is it, Herman?"

Mom's youngest son continued to stir his potatoes with his fork. "Nope. But I was wondering. all the same. You're always saying how Mrs. Hjalmer only has Ione, like you feel sorry for her. So I was curious about why she didn't have more."

"I'm not 'sorry' for her, exactly. Ione's a wonderful child..."

"Then why didn't she have more?"

"Sometimes it isn't possible, Herman."

"Why not? Most everybody we know's got more'n one kid."

Mom threw a pleading glance in Dad's direction but he refused to look at her and stared into his plate. I got the feeling that he thought the conversation was venturing into women's stuff and he wasn't going to be dragged into it.

"She coulda had a couple of boys, like you Mom. Then she wouldn't be fussin' with no wedding showers."

"Any wedding showers."

Herman was nonplussed. "Okay, any wedding showers. So how come?"

"I've said it isn't any of your business didn't I? But if you must know, after Ione, Mrs. Hjalmer couldn't have any more children."

Herman looked up from his fork as if he'd been told it was bed time. "How come? She's still married isn't she?"

"Well of course she's married."

About that time, Dad seemed to take pity on his wife. "Now you heard what your mother said. Mrs. Hjalmer has the one child and she can't have any more. That's more than you need to know so that's the end of it."

If I hadn't been so stupefied, I'd have done exactly as Herman was told to do. I'd have kept my mouth shut. But when I'd heard what my mom said, I couldn't believe my ears. Mrs. Hjalmer seemed as normal as everyone. "1-Is that true Mom? Mrs. Hjalmer can't have anymore kids?"

I could feel Uncle Henry's eyes narrowing as if he were trying to peer inside me. He didn't utter a word, but Dad did. "I thought I just told you, that's the end of it. No more talk about Mrs. Hjalmer or her family. You boys finish up your dinner. There's dishes and homework to do."

The conversation at the table came to an abrupt end. Mom seemed uncomfortable, Dad looked annoyed and Uncle Henry sat in a pensive state. For once, Herman and I were glad to escape to the kitchen, though we didn't talk about Mrs. Hjalmer, in case we were overhead. The hall clocked chimed 9 p.m. as we climbed into our beds. By then Herman had forgotten about the incident. He began reading the comic books I'd lent him with a clear conscience. But I couldn't stop thinking about our neighbor and the more I thought about what

155

I'd done to spoil her daughter's big day, the worse I felt.

Of course I gave myself plenty of excuses. I didn't mean for the vase to be broken. And how was I to know Mrs. Hjalmer made such a fuss over Ione because she couldn't have any more children? I was playing a joke, for crumb sakes. It was only a joke.

The more I tried to convince myself that I was guilty of nothing, the more I knew I was a fool. That night I dreamed about vases, all kinds of them: big ones, tall ones, hand painted ones, plain ones and all of them exploding into a million pieces and all of them needing to be glued back together again. By morning my pillow was so damp with worry that my hair stuck to my forehead, like I'd just stepped out of the swimming hole. Herman kept laughing and pointing the way he did when I'd turned green. Eventually, Mom wandered in to see what the fuss was about. She took one look at me and hurried to the medicine cabinet. That's where she kept the thermometers, one oral and one rectal. Herman hung around in case she came back with the latter, a cigar shaped instrument of torture which the Fuller Brush man had convinced her to buy in case a lock jaw epidemic ever hit our community. She came back without the jar of Vaseline required for rectal insertion so Herman lost interest in my condition and wandered downstairs.

Once I was pronounced well enough to have breakfast in the kitchen, I dawdled over my oatmeal, perching my head in one hand with my elbow jammed into the table. Dad had already left for the precinct and Mom was too busy frying eggs to tell me to sit up straight. Herman nudged me a couple of times, but I nudged back hard enough to make him quit.

"Need some honey for that oatmeal?" said Uncle Henry, staring at me the way he'd done the day before.

"No thanks," I said, avoiding his eyes in case he could read my thoughts.

156

"So, what are you boys getting up to today? Looks like another hot one. Swimming maybe?"

Herman snorted. "He's already been swimming... in his bed!"

"That so?" said our relative cocking his head. "How's that exactly?"

Mom told him she'd thought I'd had a fever but I didn't. "A case of growing pains, I expect. Anyway, he's fine." Of course she could say that because as far as I knew thermometers didn't measure a person's conscience. If they did, I'd have been sent to back to bed for sure.

"What're you doin' today, Uncle Henry? Maybe I could hang out with you."

"That would be nice, Herman. I'd like that. But not today. I got me a little job, cleaning out Harold Swanson's back storeroom. He needs space for some new supplies."

"Maybe I could help? I could sweep."

"Tell me Herman Larson," said Mom, laying Uncle Henry's plate of eggs in front of him. "Why is it you're willing to sweep floors at the hardware store, but let me ask you to do something around here and you evaporate like a fog?"

"Aw, Elsie, the boy just wants to see a bit of the world."

"Well, I'd be glad if he could see a bit of his bedroom floor first. If you want something to do, Herman, pick up all those toys and comic books you've got scattered everywhere."

"They ain't all mine!"

"Aren't. Aren't all yours."

"That's right. Most of 'em are Ollie's."

"They are not, you little creep." I could feel my face turn a sudden crimson. "I picked up my stuff yesterday. Those are your tinker toys on the floor. You're such a liar, Herman."

"Oliver!" Mom's mouth fell open and she looked at me as I'd tossed a half a dozen frogs on the table.

Maybe I was wrong to call Herman a creep, but I didn't want to hear a lecture either. A person can't be perfect all the time. Leastwise, I couldn't. "I'm outta here," I heard myself saying. Then I sprang from my chair and flew out the door. Tired of the world, I spent the day hidden among the blackberries.

Nothing was said about my behavior at dinner except Mom kept looking at me as if she thought I might be sick after all. Once or twice she felt my forehead but finding nothing wrong went on about the business of feeding her family.

Uncle Henry stared at me from across the table. "Did you have a good day, Ollie?"

Before I could answer, Dad snorted. "What could be wrong with his day, Henry? School's out, the sun's warm and there's little for him to do except his paper route and a few chores. I wish I were twelve again."

Uncle Henry tossed his brother-in-law a sober expression. "It's been a while, but I think I recall having some pretty rough days when I was a kid."

"How's that?" said Dad, looking up from his bowl of chicken noodle soup. "I never heard of anyone getting a headache from daydreaming."

"John," said Mom quietly, but with slight growl in her voice.

"Oh heck, Elsie. Henry knows I'm kidding."

"A joke's only funny if everyone's laughing."

Dad paused to think about what his wife had said. Then he nodded in agreement. "Sorry, Henry."

"No offense taken," came the reply.

After that, Dad went back to slurping his soup and saying how good it was.

A week passed and then two without much more being said about the failed wedding shower except that Mrs. Hjalmer'd gone a little peculiar. Her husband complained that she'd spread ant poison all over the house and that he had to take off his shoes and socks at the front door every day before he was allowed inside. Mrs. Hjalmer didn't want him trucking in another passel of ants.

His wife's eccentric behavior was my fault, of course, but I didn't know how to make amends. Confessing to what I'd done wouldn't calm Mrs. Hjalmer's ant obsession or bring back the cherished vase. Besides, there was my skin to think about. Nope I couldn't see any way out of my predicament even though I spent a lot of time in my hideout brooding about it.

One afternoon, near the butcher shop, I ran into Luscious Lucas. He seemed surprised to see me, like I might be a long lost relative, but fell into walking beside me as he was used to doing. He didn't say much at first, just gave me those side glances that a lot of people seemed to be doing of late. Finally his curiosity got the better of him and he asked if I'd been recovering from chicken pox. That brought me up short.

"Chicken pox?" I bawled at him. "Where'd you get that stupid notion? Do I look like I got chicken pox? Do you see scabs on my face?"

"No-o," Luscious replied cautiously, but looking me straight in the eye. "That's why I asked. We ain't seen much of you lately. Stubby said you might have chicken pox."

"Well, tell Stubby I don't have any such thing and he can quit making up stories about me. I'm fine. I'M FINE."

Luscious lagged behind when I started walking again. "I'll tell Stubby you're okay," he called out to the back of my head. His voice was a mixture of confusion and apology. "Are you coming to the ballpark Saturday?"

"No!" I was almost sprinting when I answered him, afraid Luscious would ask why. To be honest, I didn't have an answer. I just wanted to be left alone.

Saturday morning was mild. Not too hot. Not too cold. Perfect weather for a ballgame. But I paid no mind to the temperature. I was caught up in my dilemma. Everyone else's life appeared to have returned to normal. Even the ant hill at the back of the vacant lot was two feet tall again. But my life was in shambles. Because of me Mr. Hjalmer had to eat his dinner without his shoes and socks. Because of me Ione might never have a fine piece of china. And Mrs. Hjalmer would never have any more babies... which wasn't because of me, but it was true that I'd spoiled the party for her only child and left the woman terrified of ants. I felt like I had a chicken bone lodged half way in my throat. I couldn't forget my guilt but I didn't dare confess either.

The sun was high overhead when I heard someone tromping through the blackberry bushes. Whoever it was seemed to be headed for my hideout. I hunkered down so as not to be seen, but the next thing I knew, Uncle Henry had stuck his head half way into my den. I couldn't have been more surprised if a hippopotamus had wandered by and asked me the time of day.

"U-Uncle Henry, how did you find me?"

The man who was stood 6'2" folded up beside me as easy as if he were a lawn chair, his knees almost touching his chin.

"I've known about this hideout of yours for some time. Everybody needs a quiet place now and again. That's why I've never stopped by till now."

"S-So how come you're here?"

"Because I got something for you." As he spoke, he reached into his shirt pocket and pulled out an object that was heavily wrapped in tissue paper. He handed it to me with his characteristic crooked smile.

"A present? For me? But it's not my birthday or anything."

"Open it," my uncle prodded. "You'll figure out why."

Whatever was buried in all that wrapping was hard but small enough to fit into the palm of my hand. I tried to imagine what it could be as I unwound layer after layer of paper.

"Be careful with it now," Uncle Henry cautioned as I was getting to the end. "Keep a good hold of it."

A second later I saw what it was and despite my being twelve and being a boy, my eyes filled with tears.

"You knew all along, didn't you? You knew I was the one who did it?"

The man beside me shrugged. "I been with you Ollie most of your life and I think I know you pretty well. Besides, I was standing at my window the day you came tearing out of the house with the shovel and all that tissue paper."

"Do Mom and Dad know?"

Uncle Henry chuckled. "It's a strange thing about parents.

161

They're so busying raising their kids that they don't always have the time to step back and observe them. No, I don't think they do. Leastwise, they haven't said anything to me."

"What am I gonna do, Uncle Henry? I feel so bad about what happened."

"I'd say you've already taken the first step: knowing you did something wrong. The second step is to take that vase over to Mrs. Hjalmer and apologize."

"What if she tells Mom and Dad?"

"Maybe she will and maybe she won't. That's a risk you gotta take. But between you and me, Ollie, I think Mrs. Hjalmer is fonder of boys than she lets on. If you tell her you're truly sorry… "

"I am. I am."

"Then I'm guessing she'll see into your heart and won't want to get you into any more trouble. However it goes, you got to make a clean breast of it. You can't live out here among the berry bushes forever and as far as I know, pranks ain't a hanging offense."

I couldn't help smiling at what Uncle Henry had said and the goofy way he looked at me. I loved and respected my parents, but when it came to having uncles, I was probably one of the luckiest kids in Ohio.

"I-I don't have any money to pay you back..."

"You can pay me on time. Like a lay-away, out of the money from your paper route."

"Can you afford to wait that long?"

The man with smiling eyes ruffled my hair. "Looks like I'll have to. Anyway, Harold's got some more work for me at the hardware store. I'll make out. One thing's for certain, no matter what my financial situation, I'll always get a square meal. Your mother isn't going to throw me out." We grinned at one another knowing he'd spoken a truth that was gospel.

"Go on now," Uncle Henry gave me a nudge. "Get yourself across the street and make things right. That baseball team of yours needs you. I wandered over to the park a little earlier. They got Luscious playing catcher. The only thing that kid can hold on to is a hamburger."

I laughed out loud for the first time in three weeks and it felt good. I was ready to face Mrs. Hjalmer.

As it turned out, Uncle Henry was right about our neighbor.

When I told her what I'd done and how sorry I was and gave her the vase, which I said I was paying for out of my paper route money, she was so surprised that she gave me a hug instead of a tongue-lashing. A minute later, though, she was shaking a finger in my face. "These tricks of yours can backfire, Oliver Larson. Didn't Mrs. Katafias teach you anything?"

"Y-You know about my turning green?"

''Who doesn't? Maybe some Eskimo in Alaska hasn't heard of it. But he'd be the only one."

We exchanged smiles, having come to a deeper understanding and liking for one another. "I won't say anything to your parents," said Mrs. Hjalmer, leaning down as if divulge a secret. "Not if you've learned a lesson."

"I think I have ma'am. I truly have. A joke's not funny unless everyone can laugh."

Chapter 12 - The Joke That Wasn't Funny

Photograph: Hettie Maitland standing with Oliver and his baseball friends in front of her patch of sunflowers, August 1940

The summer of 1940 was the laziest I'd enjoyed in my almost thirteen years. Madison Elementary School had closed early, near the end of May, because of a problem with the roof. The gang and I couldn't have been happier as the weather was balmy and we spent the extra days on the baseball diamond at Hettie Maitland Park.

The land had been donated to the community in 1875 by Francis Pilgrim on the occasion of his daughter's marriage to Robert Maitland. Maitland had been a blacksmith who'd made a comfortable living and who'd spearheaded the formation of the town's library. The marriage had been a happy one until Hettie's husband died at the age of 57. He left his wife well provided for, however, and their three surviving sons were able to carry on with the business, though the eldest, Daniel, eventually bought out his brothers.

By 1940, Mrs. Maitland, whose home bordered the park, was 82 years-old and looked every bit her age. Her hair was white, her skin was parchment and she was bent like a banana; but she prided herself on her teeth which were white and even as a picket fence without the gaps. Our dentist, Dr. Welch, said that Hettie had strong teeth because she ate lots of vegetables. Hettie -- whom everyone addressed by her first name -- was inclined to discount the dentist's opinion. Raw milk, straight from the

165

cow was her secret.

Over the years she'd kept a series of them tethered in her back yard. Petunia was her most recent pet, a Jersey with soft brown eyes that the old woman spoiled by feeding it coffee cake from time to time. In gratitude, Petunia rewarded her owner with a generous supply of milk, enough for her to bathe in if she'd wanted.

Dr. Carlson frowned on the idea of drinking unpasteurized milk and often warned Hettie of its dangers. She'd listen to his lectures, thank him and then go on doing exactly as she liked. She said the doctor's ideas were "new fangled" and cited her good health was an argument in her favor.

Hettie used that word, "new-fangled" a lot, much to the consternation of her son, Daniel. One bright day in May, he sat drinking coffee at the Marabar diner, complaining about his mother's refusal to use the telephone he'd had installed for her. "She's had the thing a month, but will she use it? No. Either she lets it ring or she picks up the receiver and bangs it down again. Doesn't say a word."

"Did you tell her it would be good to have in case of an

emergency?" Mrs. McBride was cutting Daniel Maitland a piece of apple pie at the time.

"Course I did, Pat. You know what she says to me? 'I've lived 82 years, given birth to four sons, and buried one along side of my husband. I know enough about life to take care of myself.' "

Nobody had an argument against Hettie's self-assessment. She had seen and endured a lot of change in her life. Eventually, the conversation drifted back to talk about Germany's invasion of Belgium.

One might have thought that the goings on in Europe would have put the mechanic's complaints in perspective; but they didn't. A couple of days later, he was sitting in the diner again, telling anyone who'd listen about his on-going telephone war with his mother. "You're not gonna believe what ma said to me this morning when I dropped by. She's taken to leaving the receiver off the hook so all I get is a busy signal. When I asked why, she said it was because she didn't want strangers to seep through the wires."

"Seep through the wires? What'd she mean by it?"

"That's exactly what I wanted to know, Oscar. And you won't believe her answer. She thinks that if those wires can carry voices, they might carry people, too. Just suck 'em right through the mouth piece. 'Next thing I know,' she says, 'they'd be dumped in my living room, demanding a piece of my sunflower seed cake.'"

A general guffaw rose up among the patrons at the Marabar diner. When the laughter died down, Oscar spit out the toothpick he'd been sucking so he could offer an opinion. "She's joshing you, Daniel. She knows better. That old woman's as sharp as a tack."

"Maybe so, but she sounded serious to me."

Mr. Hartley, the mailman, spoke up next. "What about the radio? It's got wires. She listens to that doesn't she?"

Daniel Maitland shook his grey head. "I reminded her about the radio. She never misses the Fred Allen Show. I asked her why she wasn't worried that Mr. Allen might come seeping through those wires."

"And what did she say?" Mr. Hartley seemed to have taken a keen interest in the dispute.

"Well, the first thing she did was pinch me in the arm like I'd said something stupid..."

"She's all of about 97 lbs, isn't she?" Oscar snorted. "That must've hurt."

"Make all the fun you want, but those boney little fingers of hers are sharp as needles."

Mr. Hartley persisted as if he were waiting for the punch line of a joke. "But what about Fred Allen? Did she really think he might show up in her parlor?"

"She said that Mr. Allen couldn't hear through the radio, so there'd be no way for him to know where she was."

The mailman nodded with a smile of admiration. "That old girl has an answer for everything. She sure got me the other day when I brought the Sears catalogue. It had some postage due but do you think she'd pay for it? Nope. It wasn't her mistake, she said."

"So what'd ya do with it?"

"I paid the two cents and left her with it. She knew I wasn't gonna haul that big catalogue around all day."

"Told you... sharp as a tack," Oscar hooted.

Mrs. McBride stared at her customer with an eyebrow lifted, waiting for the silence to fall. "Have you ever thought, Daniel, that maybe Hettie hates that telephone because she's afraid it'll mean she'll see less of you? That you'll call her instead of going over?"

"Aw that's stupid, Pat. I go by three or four times a week. It won't be no different with the telephone."

"Then maybe you better tell her. We mothers get kinda crazy where our kids are concerned."

Daniel Maitland paused as the waitress poured him in a second round of coffee. "You might be right Pat," he grunted. ''You might be right."

Right or not, the battle between Daniel Maitland and his mother about the telephone continued to rage. He got her to leave the receiver on the cradle though, because on a warm day with her windows open, me and the guys could hear it ringing. The diamond wasn't more than 200 feet away from her white Victorian with its wrap around porch, or "stoop" as she called. But no matter how long the phone rang, she still refused to answer it. One day, we counted 42 rings, and then stopped counting because Stubby Norville hit a high fly ball into left field. Stubby hoped to be a ball player one day, just like I did, but there was one difference between us. He could hit deep in any direction almost anytime he wanted.

Anyway, Luscious was standing close in when he saw the ball headed in his direction. He started to run backwards, keeping his eye on the leather because he wanted to prove himself. We always stuck him where we were pretty sure the balls wouldn't go. He was going to catch that fly or die trying. Behind him was Hettie's hallowed sunflower patch where she collected the seeds for her famous cake. He didn't see it, of course, or he'd

169

have stopped in his tracks. He knew his priorities. After a ballgame, we could count on Hettie for tall glasses of lemonade and a slice of cake.

"Look out, Luscious," I shouted, as he continued to careen backwards. My warning came too late. He'd already cut a swath that led from left field to Hettie's side porch. As he slammed up against the house, the rest of us watched the fly ball arc and land somewhere in the back yard.

Each of us froze, expecting to see our friend and benefactor fly out the screen door to ask if the house had been hit by a hurricane; but the place remained silent. Hettie must have been on an errand, maybe to the library, which she loved, or to the dry goods store for material to make another quilt. Either way, she didn't know several of her precious sunflowers had been mowed down and no one wanted to stick around to tell her. Stubby remembered an errand he had to do for his mother. Eric went home to mow the lawn, and Luscious said he needed to feed his dog. One by one, we drifted away, trying to ease our conscience with the notion that we were needed elsewhere and hoping against hope that Hettie wouldn't notice the damage we'd done.

Of course, we couldn't have been more wrong. She'd noticed all right. Not only that but, according to Dad, who came home with the story that night, her cow, Petunia, had gone missing. The way I figured it, Stubby's ball scared the Jersey and it bolted. Anyway, the animal had found its way to Main Street and was holding up traffic with its slow meanderings. Pretty soon the drivers' nerves got frayed and by the time Dad arrived on the scene, so many horns were blaring that the shoppers had poured out on to the sidewalks to enjoy the sight of Petunia leading a motorcade.

When Dad got back to Hettie's place with the cow, her owner was standing on the porch looking like she'd crawled out of a hay stack. Her hair was sticking out of her bun and sun flower petals were nesting in it. She started yelling the moment she saw Dad approach. "I told you! I told you! Some stranger's seeped through the telephone, ruined my flowers and stolen my Petunia. Where did you find her? Was it next to a telephone?"

Dad sauntered up and tied the cow to the porch railing. "What are you going on about, Hettie? I found Petunia taking a stroll down Main Street. You didn't tie her up properly, that's all."

"Well, I'd like to believe you, John, but go round to the side of the house and you'll see someone's been here. Look at my sunflowers."

Hettie followed Dad around to the side of the house. Five or six of the golden giants lay on the ground, but aside from that there wasn't much sign of vandalism. "Maybe the cow trampled 'em when she left. Did you think of that?"

"No," said Hettie with her hands on her hips. "Because Petunia went off by the other side of the house. I could follow her tracks until she got to the street."

"Were there any other footprints?"

"No. Because strangers that seep through telephone wires don't leave footprints."

"Hettie, will you quit that? You know as well as I do that you're talking nonsense."

The old woman looked down at her shoes, black leather high tops covered in dust. "Well, what am I to think, John? That one of my neighbors ruined my sunflowers and stole my cow? I don't know anyone around here mean enough to do that. Do you, John?"

Dad could see that Hettie was upset so he led her into the house and made her a pot of chamomile tea. Once she'd settled down, he talked to her as if she were his own mother. "I can't explain the sunflowers, Hettie, but nobody stole your cow. She wandered off, that's all. If you'd have used the telephone to call the station, somebody would have told you we had the cow in custody. You got yourself worked up over nothing."

"I-I'm sorry, John. But I love that cow." Hettie wiped her eyes with her hanky.

"Fair enough. But that's no reason to go around insisting that strangers are seeping through your telephone and creating mayhem. You've got to stop fibbing, Hettie. I mean it. Keep saying crazy things like that and one of these days people are going to think you're turning peculiar. You don't want that do you?"

The old woman, who was looking sad and frail, shook her head. "No, I don't want that. I promise, I won't say it any more."

"Good," said Dad, rising to leave. "And I promise, I'll get to the bottom of the sunflower caper. Didya ever think the kids might have done it?"

Hettie's eyes opened wide. "Of course not. I love those kids as much as my Petunia. They'd never do a thing like that."

"Well, not intentionally, maybe. Anyway, I'll look into it."

When we heard Dad's account, Herman and I looked at each other like a pair of condemned prisoners. We didn't want to fess up to what we'd done but we knew we couldn't keep quiet either. It wouldn't do to have Hettie think that someone had a grudge against her. At supper, we told Dad what had happened.

"Luscious wasn't to blame," I insisted. "We never should have put him into left field where those sunflowers would go unprotected."

172

Dad listened to the whole story without interrupting. He was chewing on one of Mom's buttermilk biscuits and enjoying it. When Herman and I had finished our confession, Dad nodded to indicate he understood how the accident could have happened, but we weren't entirely out of the woods. "Didn't any of you hang around to tell Hettie you were to blame? Did you leave a note?"

"No sir," Herman answered. "W-We didn't think of it."

"Well, that's pretty poor thinking for a pair of sharp fellas. She was bound to wonder."

"We didn't know her cow had got loose," I pitched in. "If we had, we'd have gone looking for it."

Dad nodded to indicate he believed our story. "Next time, if there is one and I hope there isn't, I don't want to hear that my sons ran away like cowards. I expect you to tell the truth and take your punishment. You got that?" Dad was wagging a finger at us as Herman and I agreed. After that, he got up from the table and went to call Hettie to tell her what had happened. As usual, she didn't answer and let the telephone ring.

Frustrated, Dad came back to the table. "That has got to be the most stubborn woman on the planet." Having spoken to the air, he turned his attention to my brother and me. "Tomorrow, I want you to go over to Hettie's place and tell her the truth. Take the other boys, if you can make 'em. They owe her an apology too." Dad started to take another bite from his biscuit then stopped. "And tell that old woman I tried to call her but she wouldn't pick up the telephone."

The next day was bright and sunny, perfect for a ballgame, but Herman and I trudged over to the park for a different reason. I wasn't surprised to find most of the guys were missing. Stubby was there, and Erick and Luscious, but I saw no joy in their faces. Their eyes were red, as if they hadn't slept. When I told them what Dad had said about telling the truth, they replied that they'd come to the same conclusion. Glad that I didn't have to argue, I headed for the white Victorian with the gang following behind like ducklings.

Hettie's smile and cheerful greeting made my shoulders droop. I hated to disappoint her but I didn't like being a coward either. She heard our confession without interrupting and remained silent while she considered the matter. Meanwhile, the scent of something baking in her kitchen made my mouth water. Luscious, driven to distraction by it, was the first to break the silence.

"Would that be sunflower seed cake I smell, Hettie?"

"Why yes, it is." The old woman's face turned as bright as a new penny. "Want a piece when it's done?"

Luscious opened the screen door and stepped inside, satisfied that we were forgiven. "I'd love some. And if you have any left over lemonade?"

"I'll make it fresh," Hettie promised. Then she opened the screen door wider to let the rest of us pour in like termites to a barn raising.

Not long after, we were joined by other members of the gang who showed up for the same reason we had. Soon, Hettie's parlor was stuffed with boys making noise, sprawled out in comfortable chairs or on the floor. She couldn't have looked happier.

We didn't play baseball that day. Instead, we ate pastries and laughed in Hettie's sunny parlor. She giggled like a school girl at our silly jokes, which encouraged us to tell more.

"Why did the farmer bury money in his field?"

"Tell me, Herman. Why did he?" Hettie seemed to enjoy playing the straight man.

"Cause he wanted his soil to be rich."

Our hostess slapped her thigh in appreciation. "That's a good one. I hope I can remember it long enough to tell Daniel."

"I got one," said Eric, raising his hand as if he were in school. "What did the math book say to the history book?"

"I don't know that either. What did it say?"

"Boy, do I have problems."

Stubby wrinkled his nose. "I heard that one before. But it wasn't a history book, it was an Atlas."

"Either way," said Hettie. "It's another good joke."

The sun was high overhead before we realized how much time had elapsed. Nobody was hungry, but we all had to go home for lunch. Together, we resettled the chairs or returned the pillows we'd tossed on the floor to their proper places. Everyone was talking and laughing at the same time when, to everyone's surprise, Herman suddenly collapsed behind me. I turned to see him laying at my feet and flapping his arms like a bird with broken wings.

"Quit clowning," I snapped as I reached down to pull him up by his collar, but the kid didn't budge. He hung like a weight at the end of my arm. "Come on, Herman. We got to go home. Whatever you're playing at, it's not funny."

My brother didn't respond but started to moan as he clutched at his belly. His eyes were half-closed and watching him writhing on the floor, I got a bad feeling in the pit of my stomach. "What's the matter with ya? Are ya sick?" Herman gave me a slight nod and moaned. again. "I-I think it's my appendix," he whispered.

"Appendix? Like it might be bursting or something?" Herman nodded a second time but said nothing.

By now, Hettie was bent over the kid, feeling his forehead while the gang formed a circle over him. "I don't feel no temperature," she said. "But maybe one of you boys better run to Dr. Carlson's and tell him to come over, right away."

"Why don't you call him?" said Stubby. "It's quicker."

"Yeah, I know the number," Luscious added. "555. Mama calls him all the time."

Hettie looked over at the telephone as if it were a snake coiled up in her parlor.

"Never mind. I'll do it," I heard myself growl. I started to rise but Herman latched on to me and refused to let go.

"Don't leave me, Ollie," he said, "I'm scared. I'm awful scared."

Afraid to move, my eyes locked on to those of the old woman's. I didn't need to say a word. She sprang to her feet as if someone had yelled "Fire!" Half a second later, she'd grabbed that receiver by the throat, hard enough to strangle it, and started dialing. Apparently, the rotary didn't move fast enough to suit her because she was shouting into the mouthpiece before Dr. Carlson came on the line. "You got to come over. You got to come over quick."

"Hettie? Is that you?"

"Yes, it's me. I got a sick boy here. You got to come quick."

"You don't have to shout. I can hear you well enough."

"Then come over ya fool!" She slammed down the telephone and rushed back to Herman's side. "He's comin', my darlin' boy. He'll be here any minute. Don't you worry. Nothin' bad's gonna happen. I'll fight the devil hisself if I have to." Then she took hold of Herman's other hand and hung on to it as if he might drift out to sea if she were careless. She was crying, too, silent tears that slid along the creases of her eyes and down to her chin.

Minutes later, though it seemed an eternity, Dr. Carlson came bounding up the porch stairs, his black bag bouncing at his side. He didn't have to ask who the patient was. My brother was still on the floor. He stared up at the doctor with a face the color of home plate. "Where does it hurt, Herman?" The man with the shaggy grey hair was pulling a stethoscope from his bag as he spoke. If he'd have bothered to look his patient in the eye, he'd have seen the confusion in my brother's eyes.

"He's been holding his stomach," Hettie answered for him.

By now Dr. Carlson was examining my brother in earnest. He listened to his heart. Took his temperature and then poked his extended belly. "What have you been feeding these boys?" he asked Hettie as he observed the number of crumb filled trays scattered about the room. "Too many sweets, I suspect", he said answering his own question. "Herman's got a stomach ache. That's all."

"You're sure it's not his appendix? He said he thought it was his appendix."

"Yes, but he's not the doctor, is he? You've got to stop feeding these boys as if they were geese meant for the Christmas table."

"I didn't mean no harm..."

"And no real harm's been done, if you can believe a 'fool'."

Hettie's face crumpled like a used napkin. "I-I'm sorry for what I said. I was scared, that's all."

"Well, one good thing's come out of it. You had the sense to use the telephone." Dr. Carlson got to his feet and pulled Herman up after him.

"I'll take the Larson boys home. A little bed rest and some cod liver oil will work miracles."

When she heard the doctor, Hettie started to cry again. This time her tears were joyful ones.

Though it wasn't much past noon, Mom put my brother to bed as soon as he got home. She forced not one but two tablespoons of cod liver oil down him, which he had to swallow without orange juice or even water. She was afraid to put any thing else into his tummy. Poor Herman, I felt so sorry for him and handed him my latest Captain Marvel comic book, the one I hadn't yet read.

At supper, Mom took some chicken soup up to him, which looked a whole lot better than the broccoli that was lying limp on my plate. Uncle Henry was quiet that night but Dad kept shaking his head, amazed that Hettie had been the one to call the doctor.

"That'll make Daniel happy and maybe put an end to their arguments."

Later, after beating Uncle Henry at two games of checkers, I went upstairs. I figured Herman could use the company. He was sitting up in his bed wearing a doleful expression when I entered.

"What's the matter? Aren't you feeling any better?"

He nodded to indicate that he was, but he didn't look at me nor did he seem interested in my comic book that was lying open on his lap. His eyes were on the closet door across the room. I couldn't see anything of interest there except a poster of Jimmie Fox of the Boston Red Sox. I'd hung it on the door the previous year.

"What are ya lookin' at?"

"Nothin'," Herman muttered. "I been thinkin' is all."

"Thinkin'?" I snorted. "Want to give yourself a headache, too?"

Herman swiveled his eyes in my direction. "It's not funny, Ollie. I feel bad about somethin' and I don't know what to do."

"Bad about what?"

"I can't tell ya. I promised Uncle Henry."

"Promised what?"

"I just said I couldn't tell ya, didn't I?"

"Listen Herman, don't bring up a thing and refuse to finish it. Whatever you promised Uncle Henry, it doesn't matter. You've already half broke your word by saying you've got a secret. Now what is it?"

"Y-you won't say anything to anyone else? Not even Uncle Henry?"

I made a crisscross over my heart with my right hand. "Hope to die. Now tell me."

"I-I wasn't sick this afternoon. I was play acting."

"What? You were flopping all over the floor like a fish on dry land."

"I know. I know. But that's what Uncle Henry said I should do."

"Why? You scared the pants off everybody. Why would Uncle Henry want you to do that?"

"He said I should scare Hettie so she'd use the telephone. That's why I took hold of your hand and wouldn't let go. I was supposed to get Hettie to call."

"So you made her phone the doctor for nothing? Wasted his time?"

"Don't make it sound so bad. Uncle Henry said she needed to make her peace with that telephone. Her son couldn't talk sense into her. But maybe she'd see the use of it if there was an emergency."

"You, for example?"

"Well, yeah. That was the idea."

"You know, Herman," I said, exasperated. "You deserved those two doses of cod liver oil. You had everybody in lather. Now it turns out you were telling a lie."

"I know. I know. That's what makes me feel so bad. I was trying to help Hettie, but I guess I didn't think it through."

"Neither you or Uncle Henry. This has got to be his craziest caper."

"But what can I do about it? I feel so guilty. What I did wasn't right, but it was for Hettie. Uncle Henry and I were afraid she might be sick and alone one day and not even know the doctor's number. Maybe not even know how to dial her son. Did ya ever think of that, Ollie?"

I was forced to admit that I hadn't. Till then, like every one else, I'd made a joke of Hettie's eccentricity. But the way my little brother put it and the anguish in his expression made me see there was more to the telephone war than I suspected. I understood why Daniel Maitland got so worked up about his mother and why Herman and Uncle Henry felt obliged to act. Maybe the rest of us were the ones who hadn't thought things through.

As Herman's eyes filled with tears, I went over to him and gave him a hug. "Listen, you did what you thought was right. That's all a person can do."

"But I lied. You know what Mom and Dad would say about that."

"Yeah, maybe I do. Then again, maybe I don't. It's true our folks try to show us right from wrong, but I've come to suspect that things aren't always as black and white as our parents make out. What you did for Hettie was follow your heart. Who knows? One day your little joke may end up saving her life. You've done nothing to be ashamed of. I'm proud of you, Lash. Really proud."

Chapter 13 - A Lesson Learned

Photograph: Herman and his best friend, Derrick Larkin, drinking cocoa in our kitchen, September 1940

I didn't have a flea-brained notion about what I was going to do, but I was mad -- madder than I'd ever been. All I knew was that I had to get rid of my little brother! For the past two weeks, Herman had stuck to me like a tick. Why, I didn't know. He wasn't a baby. He was in the second grade, for crumb sakes! When I complained to Mom, she shrugged and called it a phase.

I was standing in the kitchen at the time, waiting for the first batch of her sugar cookies to come out of the oven. Mom said it was too near supper for me to be thinking of sugar cookies and ordered me out of the room so I wouldn't be underfoot.

"What about Herman? He's always underfoot," I moaned.

Mom put down her cookie cutter and looked me straight in the eye. "I expect he's lonely, Oliver, with Derrick being so ill..."

Derrick was Herman's friend and at the mention of his name, I realized I hadn't seen the little guy for a while. "What's wrong with Derrick? I didn't know he was sick."

"Mrs. Larkin thought it was the flu and so did Dr. Carlson at first, but now the doctor wants Derrick to go to Columbus for some tests. She's taking him today on the four o'clock train. Some of these cookies are for them, so don't wander off. You can run them over when they're ready."

183

The strain in Mom's voice was unmistakable. I knew she could wear other people's troubles like a winter coat. But what was she afraid of? What could be so wrong with a kid who was eight years old?

A cascade of red and yellow leaves was falling as I stepped onto the porch. No one was in sight except the postman, and he was half way up the block delivering the afternoon mail. As it was Saturday, I thought about wandering over to the Bake Shoppe to see if any of the gang was around, but dismissed the idea as I would soon be needed for Mom's errand. Her news had left me feeling empty. Derrick was a nice kid: gullible enough to be the butt of my beautiful jokes and amiable enough to take no offense.

In contrast to my little brother who was stocky, blonde and freckled, Derrick was delicate, like his mother, with a bounty of dark curls encircling his pale face. He always played an angel in the Christmas pageants and though he was often teased for being the "teacher's pet," he was never offended. All the attention, he knew, was a compliment. Everyone liked Derrick Larkin.

Instead of walking toward town, I headed in the opposite direction, toward the Marabar diner, which was only a few blocks away. I figured I'd have an hour to spend before the cookies were out of the oven and cool enough to handle. Maybe I'd find Dad in one of the booths, taking a break from his rounds. He often stopped there to listen to the farmers complain about the price of corn or what the scoundrels in the Ohio legislature were doing to affect wheat prices. Boring talk, I called it; Dad called it the voice of the heartland.

I was barely half way down the block when I heard our front door slam. Herman was on my trail. I didn't have to turn around to know he was racing to catch up with me.

"Go home, Herman. I'm busy," I said, without looking back.

"Busy doin' what?"

I didn't like his tone or the fact that he was close enough for me to see him out of the corner of my eye. "None of your bee's wax." My strides got longer, but Herman managed to keep up.

"I heard Mom say you was to stay home."

"No, she didn't."

"Sure she did."

"Didn't."

"Okay, so where are we going?"

"WE aren't going anywhere, Herman. I'M going to the diner." I jammed my fists into my pockets rather than rap my kid brother behind the ear. One pocket contained something round and hard, a dime I had stashed there and forgotten. "I'm going to buy a Lime Rickey," I said with a new confidence. "So unless you've got money on you, go home. Oscar doesn't like kids hanging around unless they buy something."

Under normal circumstances, my pronouncement would have earned a belly laugh. Herman always had more money than I did. But by the time he ran home for it, I could ditch him. Maybe I wouldn't go to the Marabar. Herman's face puckered as if he couldn't decide whether to run home or to stick with me. Any minute now he was likely to cry. But I didn't feel sorry for him. The last couple of weeks, he'd been making my life miserable.

"So long, Herman," I said, sauntering off with a whistle. His eyes seemed to burn a hole into the back of my head. He'd probably take his revenge by short-sheeting my bed or grinding crackers in it. I didn't care so long as I could savor the moment. Heading for the Marabar, I felt like Pinocchio when he broke free of his strings.

Most of the counter stools were taken when I reached the diner. A row of men in overalls sat hunched over their coffee, but my dad wasn't among them. Homer Nordling grunted an acknowledgement as I swung on to the last stool beside him. Oscar, the proprietor, wasn't half so friendly. "Your dad left fifteen minutes ago," he said, leaning against the cash register with a spatula in his hand.

"I'm not here to see my dad, sir. I'm here to buy me a Lime Ricky."

"A Lime Ricky? On a cold day like this?"

"You're right," I agreed, slapping my dime upon the counter. "Think I'll have me a cup of coffee instead."

Oscar snorted and Homer gave me a lopsided grin. Both men knew I wasn't allowed coffee.

"Ya mean cocoa don'tcha you, Ollie?" The proprietor headed for the cocoa machine without waiting for my answer.

"Yes, sir. That's what I meant." My chest crumpled.

Oscar came back with a steaming mug and eyed the dime I had laid on the counter. Satisfied it wasn't a slug, he threw it into the till, then watched as I swallowed some of the watery liquid. Oscar's cocoa wasn't a patch on my mom's and if I'd have had my druthers, I'd have stuck with the Lime Ricky. Still, the drink was warm and I could rub my hands against the crockery the way the men at the counter did. Once they were satisfied my business was settled, their conversation drifted back to matters of concern to them.

"I hear there's money in soy beans." The man who had spoken shifted his eyes back and forth along the row of stools as if he expected to be ridiculed. Homer didn't disappoint him. "The idea's about as sensible as using spit for irrigation." He laid an arm across the man's shoulder and went on. "What's put that idea into your head, Morton? That dark-eyed gypsy girl been readin' your tea leaves again?" General laughter followed.

"She ain't no gypsy." Morton's cheeks became the color of port wine. "She's a former circus entertainer..."

"Well, whatever she is," Homer interrupted, "she should stick to advice about your love life... such as it is. She might help you with that; but she sure in HELL don't know nothin' about farmin'."

"Watch your language, Homer Nordling! There's a child present." Mrs. McBride emerged from the kitchen with a fresh pot of coffee. "I should think a man your age would know better."

"What?" Homer stared at her, wide-eyed. "What did I say?"

"You know what you said. Don't pretend otherwise."

"What's wrong with that word, woman? It's in the Bible, isn't it?"

Mrs. McBride slapped the pot down on the counter so she could look the blasphemer in the eye. "Are you claiming to know the Bible, Homer? It comes as a REVELATION!"

The promoter of soy beans chuckled, as did the others seated at the counter. Homer's ears turned a beet red but he refused to back down before the pretty widow.

"Of course, I know the Bible, woman! Didn't my momma read passages to me every night when I was little?"

Mrs. McBride picked up the coffee pot and poured some of the brown liquid into Homer's cup. "That so? And who's the lucky lady that reads it to you now?"

"There ain't no lady..." Homer caught the gleam in the waitress's eye. "Are you saying I can't read, woman? Is that it?"

"Listen, Homer Nordling," said Mrs. McBride as she leaned across the counter, "I don't know anyone in this establishment who's called 'woman'. If you're referring to me, I have a name and you'd best use it. "

The large man in overalls recoiled. He would have been a formidable opponent to anyone of his sex. But Mrs. McBride wasn't of his sex.

"Aw Pat, you know I don't mean anything. I'm sorry." Then he looked down at me. "And I apologize to you, Ollie for... well, for that word."

Mrs. McBride seemed to speak for both of us when she said he was forgiven. Then she removed a slice of apple pie from the display case and set it before her Goliath. "It's on the house. And in case you were wondering, we're still on for tonight."

Everyone sat quiet, smiling to themselves, until a stranger entered the cafe bringing a blast of wind and leaves with him. The stubble on his chin said he hadn't shaved for a couple of days and it didn't look as if he'd had much sleep either. He ordered a hamburger "to go" then kept glancing at his watch as he waited. He wanted to know what the driving conditions were like going west and volunteered that he was headed for Indiana. Oscar told him a truck driver had been through a few hours earlier who'd reported that twenty miles past Springfield the roads were flooded by the rain.

The stranger's shoulders dropped. He shook his head and headed for the door. Mrs. McBride called out to him about the hamburger so he came back and threw a few coins on the counter. Said he couldn't wait. Then he was gone.

Oscar went over to the window and peered through a curtain. "New York. That's what the license plate says. Wonder what he's doing driving to Lafayette in weather like this."

"What kind of car is it?" Morton Boeglin asked.

"Cadillac. A new one, too."

"That's a good car. But it ain't meant for weather like this." "Wonder why he's in such a hurry?" Oscar was still at the window looking out.

"Maybe he's robbed a bank."

"That's not funny, Morton. Anyone can see the man's troubled," said Mrs. McBride. "Maybe someone's sick or dying."

"One thing's certain," said Oscar, returning to the kitchen. "If he is a bank robber, he's the best dressed bank robber I ever clapped eyes on. Did you see that diamond he was wearing and those clothes? Those weren't off the rack."

"Just shows that trouble can come to anyone at any time." Mrs. McBride, who'd lost her husband in a traffic accident two years earlier, was speaking from experience. A silence fell while those present sat remembering her loss and maybe a loss of their own. Homer spoke for everyone when he said he hoped the man in the Cadillac had a safe journey and that his trouble, whatever it was, would come out right.

Eventually, Oscar noticed that my cup of cocoa had run dry. "You glued to that seat, Ollie, or what?"

"N-no, sir. I was just going. I got an errand to do at home."

Oscar took the mug away and wiped the counter clean is if to erase all trace of me. "Well, don't keep your folks waiting," he said as he peered down through his thick glasses. I was sliding off the vinyl seat, when Herman came crashing through the door. He'd been home to get his money and looked relieved to discover I was where I'd said I'd be. In a way, I was glad to see him because his arrival made my exit easy.

"Where ya goin'?" he pouted as I headed for the door.

"Nowhere," I replied.

"Then why are you in such a hurry?"

"Because I don't want you to follow."

"Why not?"

"Because I'm busy, that's why."

"Doin' what?"

By now we were standing on the sidewalk where the leaves were piled hip high against the curb. I tossed a handful of them in his direction, then started to run. Herman came after me, his face looking like it was covered with muddy brown frosting. I had to stop and laugh.

"It's not funny," he said, catching up to me. "I wouldn't do that to you."

"Then don't follow me like a stray dog. Honestly, Herman, sometimes you're such a dunce."

My little brother stood with his boots planted like stumps into the ground. "If that's true, then how come I get better grades than you? How come?"

"Because," I bawled, thrusting my face into Herman's, "the

second grade's easy. Wait till you get to the sixth grade. You'll see. There's geography and DI-VI-SION and a whole lot of junk you haven't heard of."

"Mrs. Duncan says you were a goof-off when you were in her class."

"Ah, what does Mrs. Duncan remember? She taught me four years ago. She's probably senile by now."

"Mrs. Duncan ain't senile."

"Must be if she thinks you're a good student. Now leave me alone. I got work to do."

"What kind of work?"

"Man's work. That's what."

Now it was Herman's turn to laugh.

"You ain't no man. Daddy don't even let you drink coffee. You drink milk. Same as me!"

"Is that right?" I answered, jamming my fists into my hips. "Well, it just so happens that I had me a cup of coffee not five minutes ago."

"Did not!" said Herman, too sure of himself for his own good.

"Was Daddy there?"

"No, he wasn't!" I started to walk away but Herman was intent upon having the last word.

"You're a liar, Ollie. Oscar wouldn't give you no coffee. He knows you can't have it. Anyway, you said you was getting a Lime Rickey. "

"I changed my mind."

Doubt began to crinkle the comers of Herman's eyes. "Dad's gonna be mad."

"Not if you don't rat on me." I turned and gave my little brother a threatening look that sent him back a few paces.

"Can I come with you then?"

"I m going home, you little baby."

"I ain't no baby."

"No? Then how come Mom had to put you on the potty last night? You wet your bed, didn't you?"

"That was an accident."

"Sure it was. That's what all babies say!"

"I ain't no baby!" Herman's cheeks were red and his lower lip was trembling. In a minute he would be crying, but I didn't care. The more my little brother clung to me the more I wanted to drive him away.

"Baby! Baby! Baby! I wonder if Derrick knows you're a bed wetter. I wonder if he'd still want to be your friend if he did. Maybe I should tell him, Herman. Yeah, I think he should know!"

"You shut up! Don't tell Derrick anything. He's sick. He's awful sick."

"Yeah, sick of you! Just like me! We're both sick of you!"

A light died in Herman's eyes when I said that. He backed away in measured steps as if I were a rabid dog he didn't want to excite; then, with the distance too great for me to catch up with him, he beat a trail in the direction of the precinct where our father worked. His sobs found their way back to me.

Part of me felt sorry for what I'd said; but a darker part pushed back. Wasn't Herman on his way to rat on me? Isn't that what he always did? Why should I feel sorry for a tattletale? What he deserved was a trouncing!

Mom had a rule about keeping conversations pleasant at meal times, so I didn't expect to hear any complaints about my behavior at the supper table. Of course there were signs that a storm was brewing. Dad sat with his lips stretched tight across his face and Mom scarcely looked at me except to ask if I wanted a second glass of milk. Herman was the dead giveaway. He kept swinging his legs under the table as if he hadn't a care in the world. I wanted to throttle him then and there. Too bad Uncle Henry sat between us.

After the dishes, which Herman and I finished in silence because Mom was puttering in the kitchen, I was summoned to the living room. Uncle Henry vacated his seat beside the fireplace as I entered and went upstairs. He never liked to see either Herman or me get into trouble. My little brother slipped into his empty seat but Dad shooed him away. Said he was to finish his homework in the kitchen. Herman's face curdled, but he dragged himself to his feet, pausing long enough in the doorway to stick his tongue out at me. Then it was just Dad and me.

"I hear you spent time at the Marabar today," he began. His voice was calm but that didn't mean anything. Some of my worst debacles started that way. Given enough rope, I usually hung myself. Mom came in and sat down in Uncle Henry's chair. I hoped her presence would reduce the tension, but it didn't.

"Yes sir, I was at the Marabar," I answered at last. "Mom had an errand for me so I was killing time 'til then."

"Herman says you were having a cup of coffee. Is that how you kill time? Disobeying your parents?"

"I wasn't drinking coffee. If Herman says that he's a liar!"

"No need to raise your voice, Oliver. Your mother and I aren't deaf."

"But I wasn't drinking coffee. Honest!"

"Then why would Herman say that you were?" My dad looked to my mom for support and she nodded that it was a fair question.

"Because he's a liar," I repeated. "See Mom. See why I don't want him following me around? All he does is tell tales."

"I do not!" Herman stood in the doorway, his face puffed with anger. "You know you had coffee. You said so."

"You're crazy, Herman, you know that. Why would I make up a story that was bound to get me into trouble? Everyone knows you're the world's biggest tattletale. Even Derrick says so."

"He never did. Derrick and I are friends. You're the liar! You are!"

"Stop it, the pair of you!" Dad shot up from his chair. "I won't have this ruckus. Herman. Go to your room and stay there. I don't want to hear another peep out of you!"

"B-B-u-t, Ollie's not tellin' the truth. He did have coffee. He did!"

Dad's index finger pointed toward the stairs. "You heard me!"

"Everyone's heard you, John, even the hibernating bears!"

Uncle Henry's voice floated down from the upper floor like a solitary snowflake. The effect, however, was more akin to the crack of a gun shot. Dad braced himself as though he'd been hit, then turned to blame my mother for her relative's behavior. "I won't have it, Elsie. I won't be mocked in my own house."

"He's not mocking you, John," Mom said, rising to stand beside her husband in an effort to calm him. "It's just that... well, it was only a cup of coffee."

"Yes, coffee today, but what tomorrow, Elsie? Either a parent's word is respected or it isn't. What's worse, one of our boys is lying. Is that okay?"

"No, it isn't John..."

"Then let me handle this and tell that brother of yours to mind his own affairs."

"He won't say anything more... WILL YOU, HENRY?" Mom's voice rose to address the figure crouched at the top of the stairs. Uncle Henry, who could withstand any rebuke from my father, was putty where my mother was concerned. He headed for his room in the attic without another word, though when he'd reached the safety of the third floor landing, he broke into a vigorous rendition of "The Battle Hymn of the Republic."

My father waited a moment for his annoyance to subside before taking up my transgression again. "You're telling me that Herman made up this story about the coffee? Is that what you're saying, Oliver?"

"Yes sir, it is." My eyes were wide enough to pass a barge through. "You can ask Oscar if you want. He'll tell you. I had cocoa. Herman's being a brat."

His confidence shaken, Dad sank into his chair. "I don't understand. It's not like your brother to make up a story out of thin air. What could have gotten into him?"

●

195

Mom returned to Uncle Henry's chair opposite Dad's. "It could have something to do with Derrick Larkin. The poor boy's been ill for so long and now he's off in Columbus. Maybe Herman's angry about the loss. They're such good friends..."

Dad peered at me as he mulled over Mom's idea. "You're absolutely certain, Oliver, that there's no truth to Herman's story? Do you swear it was cocoa and not coffee you had at the Marabar, because coffee's not good for a boy your age? It could stunt your growth. You don't want to be a midget, do you?"

"No sir, I don't. And I'm not lying. It was cocoa."

Dad's chin dropped into his chest with a sigh. "Well, Elsie, you could be right. What do you suppose we should do?"

Mom motioned for me to go upstairs. "Your father and I need to talk," she said. I started to leave but she stopped me by putting her hand out to catch mine. "Pay some attention to your little brother, Oliver. You're his own flesh and blood, remember, and with Derrick so ill, it's natural that he'd turn to you."

"I'll try," I told her. My voice was solemn as a vicar's, but inside, I was all confetti and streamers. I had out-maneuvered my little brother! Heck, I was so pleased with myself that I wanted to break out into "The Battle Hymn of the Republic" like Uncle Henry.

Too bad for Herman that he stuck to his story into the next day, even after Oscar corroborated that I'd been given cocoa. "Maybe Oscar's lying, too," he screamed. "Maybe Ollie paid him to say that!"

Convinced that these fibs had to be punished, Mom sent Herman to bed that evening without a slice of pineapple upside down cake. Watching him drag his feet up the stairs, I almost felt sorry for the little guy.

Two days later, Dad came home early. I was sitting in the living room with a geography book on my lap. I wasn't reading. I was pretending because Herman wasn't allowed to pester me if I was studying. The frown on my dad's face brought me to my feet. Maybe my half-truth about the coffee had been discovered.

Dad's eyes scanned the room, barely noticing me. "Where's your brother?" he asked. I told him that Herman was upstairs doing his homework. That seemed to satisfy him. He headed for the kitchen and I followed until he waved me back. "Stay put, Oliver. I need to speak to your mother."

From the hallway, I could hear him talking but I couldn't make out the words. I was sure it was about Herman. He'd been in a fight during recess. Maybe Dad had heard about it. Maybe Mrs. Duncan had dropped by the precinct.

Suddenly, Mom cried out, "Oh no, John! No!"

I'd never heard my mom's voice so anguished. Dad was murmuring softly, like he was trying to calm her. His tone frightened me more than my mother's cry. Whatever had happened, it was bad. Real bad.

Mom finally emerged, pale faced, from the kitchen. Dad was at her side, his mouth pulled down at the corners. "We have to tell you something, Oliver." She guided me into the living room and in the lamp light I could see the tears in her eyes.

"What's happened? What's wrong?"

"Sit down, Oliver. I'm afraid there's bad news from Columbus..."

"About Aunt Enid, Mom?' Is she sick?"

"No, Oliver. Your aunt's fine. It's about Derrick Larkin. He died this morning."

"Died?" I thought my mother must be crazy. I almost laughed. How could Derrick Larkin die? He was eight-years-old, for crumb sake! People didn't die when they're eight years old!

"It's called 'leukemia,'" my mother went on. "There's no cure for it. None at all..." Her voice trailed off as she reached for the hanky in her apron. "He went so fast."

Mom was crying so hard that Dad took over. "It's going to be a shock to your brother, Oliver. You'll have to help him through this, son. We all will."

"You mean the doctors let him die? They didn't do anything?" "Lower your voice, Oliver. I don't want Herman to know yet. He and Derrick were like brothers."

I buried my face in my hands realizing that lately I hadn't been much of a friend to Herman, much less a brother. I was ashamed. How could I help him? Why would he trust me?

"I don't know what to do, Dad," I said, shaking my head. "I don't know..."

His large hand patted my shoulder. "You'll know when the time comes. You're his real brother, after all."

My parents headed for the stairs. Dad had his arm about Mom's shoulders and they walked in perfect unison. Seeing them give strength to one another gave strength to me. Any hardship, I realized, could be endured with the love and support of the family. I knew I couldn't fail my little brother. When the time was right, I'd tell the truth about the coffee. I wasn't going to lie to Herman ever again -- leastwise, not to hurt him.

Chapter 14 - Mr. Papadopoulos' Pupil

Photograph: *Mr. Papadopoulos gives an impromptu recital in our livening room, November 1940*

Mr. Papadopoulos was a brilliant musician. He lived in our community during the concert off-season as a guest of our neighbors, Mr. and Mrs. Katafias. They had known him as a boy in Greece, and when he came to this country as a thirteen-year-old protégé, they took him under their wing. That was around the turn of the century. By the time I got to know him in 1940, he was in his mid fifties and by his unkempt appearance, he seemed to be a man who was disillusioned with life.

Nevertheless, when he practiced his violin in the afternoons, his music poured through our windows with all the beauty of sunlight. Mom would pause at her work at the kitchen sink, smile and get a faraway look in her eyes. Even my kid brother, Herman thought the music was "Okay."

I liked it too, and thanks to Mr. Papadopoulos, names like Beethoven, Bach and Brahms became as familiar to me as my baseball heroes, Babe Ruth, Lou Gehrig and Pinky Higgins. I was grateful to be acquainted with these legends, but what puzzled me was why a man who could create so much beauty seemed to be miserable. I asked Mom about him once, and she answered that artists were inclined to have tormented spirits. They expressed their emotions through their art and that took a lot out of them.

"I guess you could say artists are more sensitive than most," she

201

concluded.

"You mean they're sissies?" I reached for a slice of the apple she was peeling for her pie.

"No!" she said, slapping my hand away. "Being sensitive doesn't mean a person's a sissy. Where'd you get that idea? It means a person has deep feelings and cares about people."

"Is Dad sensitive?"

Mom put down her paring knife and stared at me as if I was some strange child who had wandered into her kitchen. "Of course he is. You know that. Isn't he always looking out for people? Didn't he drive Mr. Katafias to the doctor yesterday when the old man was feeling poorly?"

"Yeah. He likes to help out. But I don't think Dad's unhappy."

"Unhappy!" This time Mom jammed both fists into her hips. "Of course he's not unhappy. What a thing to say. Why he has you and your brother and Uncle Henry..."

"Uncle Henry doesn't make Dad happy."

"Oh, Oliver, you mustn't make too much of the skirmishes between my brother and your father. They don't amount to anything. They get along pretty well considering their differences. Why are you going on about your father being unhappy?"

"It's 'cause you said artists were sensitive and had tormented souls."

"Oh that!" Mom laughed. "Well, your father's no artist, is he? I can't even get him to paint our picket fence. He's been promising for two years and it's still not done. What I said was a figure of speech. You'll understand when you're older."

I hated it when grown-ups pulled out that old saw about being older. I was twelve and three quarters, for crumb sakes! How old did I have to be?

Mom started tossing flour around for her pie crust so I decided to head for the baseball diamond where the rules of the game were clear. A few of the guys were standing around when I arrived but there weren't enough of us to make a team. It was too cold. Nobody had any money to spend at the Bake Shoppe so we hung around trying to impress one another with half truths. That's when Eric Ladde said he was pretty certain that some of the girls in our class were beginning to have their periods.

For a minute, nobody dared to breathe or even snicker. Each of us waited for the other guy to expose his ignorance. Finally, Luscious Lucas helped us out.

"W-What's a 'period?'" His eyes rolled across our faces as if he feared it might be contagious. To be honest, it was a fair question. Luscious had no brothers or sisters to clue him in and as he was as round as he was tall, he didn't get much female attention. Still, none of us showed him mercy. We snorted and slapped our thighs as if his ignorance could fill an ocean. Once we'd recovered ourselves, however, we discovered that our collective wisdom wasn't enough to fill a pitcher's mitt. Arguments ensued about when, how often and why periods occurred. No one knew for certain -- not well enough to swear on a Bible -- so on that rarest of occasions, we abandoned the baseball field and headed for the library.

Once we arrived, the majority of us agreed to stay outside as we didn't want to call too much attention to ourselves. Me, Luscious, Erik and Stubby Norville, the tallest boy in our class, were elected to go in. Of course, the minute I entered I started to laugh. I don't know why, but silence always made me giggle, like a belch I could feel growing in the pit of my stomach and couldn't stop. Herman said I laughed when I was in the library because I was allergic to learning, and he might have been right. Each fall, before school started, I was famous for breaking out in hives.

Certainly, there was nothing about our library that might be considered humorous -- not the mural with its historical figures peering down from the ceiling, their arms flaying with impassioned speech, not the sound of my footsteps on the stone tiles and certainly not the sour expression of Miss Berenson, the librarian, who felt that books were wasted on the young. Nonetheless, once the door closed behind me, my shoulders started to quake. Luscious, fearing a contagion, slapped his hand over his mouth, but too late! Miss Berenson heard my snicker and snapped a cold eye in our direction. Stubby Norville was furious.

"Knock it off, Larson. Ya wanna get us kicked outta here?"

The threat had its desired effect. We filed past the information desk with the sobriety of patients in line for a rabies shot. We were lucky enough to make it as far as the section marked "human anatomy" before Luscious lost control and giggled into his hand to stifle the noise. I was grinning from ear to ear, but I was quiet, a distinction that Erik and Stubby failed to notice.

"You two are being stupid!" Stubby snapped as Luscious and I followed the pair of them behind a row of books. But when we reached the section where we were headed everyone forgot about decorum and started elbowing his neighbor for the best place to stand.

The scuffle must have aroused Miss Berenson's suspicions because she appeared like an apparition at the far end of the bookshelf.

"What are you boys up to? What are you looking for?" Her wire-rimmed glasses flashed in the light that was streaming in from the window. That flash and the row of pencils jutting like spikes from her bun made her look fierce as an Indian Warrior. So did the frown that cut vertical ruts in her forehead.

"Ah, ah... cookbooks. We're looking for cookbooks." Under her strict gaze, Luscious had melted like butter in a frying pan.

"Cookbooks?" The librarian's voice rose above her customary whisper.

"You're in the wrong section. Cookbooks are over there!" Her plump finger pointed to the far side of the room, a distance that might as well have been Siberia or the far-flung corners of Tibet as far as we were concerned. Yet what choice had we but to follow her like manacled prisoners into that distant exile?

At last, she stopped at a section marked "Culinary Arts," and pointed to a row of books above our heads. Wagging her finger at us she uttered a stern warning that we should not mess with the Dewey Decimal system.

"I'll be watching!" was her parting comment.

Left to ourselves in the cooking section, Erik slapped Luscious with his cap on the side of the head.

"Ow! What did ya do that for?"

"Cause you're a dunce, that's why. Look where you've got us! How're we gonna get back to the other side of the room?"

"It's not my fault. You guys should have said something."

"I would have if you hadn't opened your mouth! Cooksbooks, for gosh sakes! All you think about is food. "

"Do not!"

"Do too!"

"Quit it, you guys!" Stubby's growl brought everyone to attention. "What we need is a plan that gets us back where we were."

"What we need's a miracle," snapped Erik, as he gave Luscious a last shove. "Thanks to this goofus, we might as well be on the moon."

Everyone knew Erik was right. We'd have to be invisible to get across the room without being caught. We should have given up the caper but nobody wanted to tell the guys waiting outside that we'd failed. Instead, we slouched against the stacks, our bodies curved like hopeless question marks waiting for an idea.

"I know!" Luscious piped up, his eyes bright as a squirrel's. "We could be like commandoes! We could slide across the room on our bellies. Old four eyes couldn't see us that close to the ground."

Stubby and I were stunned into silence. But not Erik.

"Oh, that's brilliant," he sneered. "And if someone catches us writhing on the floor, what do we say? We got bellyaches from reading too many cake recipes!"

Stubby and I couldn't hide our sniggers, but Luscious wasn't deterred.

"Then one of us has to create a diversion. That way the others can sneak by."

Erik looked as if he were about to brain Luscious for a third time, but I intervened. "Wait a minute! Wait a minute. The kid's got an idea! Stubby, you go up and talk to Miss Berenson. Ask her a question. Yeah! And while she's answering, the rest of us can sneak back across the room, on our bellies if we have to."

"That's crazy. She's bound to see you guys. And anyway, what am I supposed to say?"

"Ask her when girls get their periods," said Luscious. That time we all gave him a swipe on the head, but we agreed to his plan. Stubby, being the tallest and most likely to block Miss Berenson's view, strolled down the center aisle, his thumbs hitched into the pockets of his jeans as though he hadn't a care in the world. The nearer he got to the information desk, however, the slower was his pace.

Miss Berenson pretended not to see him at first so he coughed. That made her head swing round.

"May I help you?" Her tone was sour enough to curdle milk.

"I need a book," Stubby answered.

"What kind of book?"

"A book about...baseball."

"Good one, Stubby," Erik whispered close to my ear.

"Fact or fiction?" Miss Berenson inquired.

"What?"

"Do you want to read about the lives of ball players, or do you want imaginary stories?"

Stubby didn't hesitate. "About real players, of course."

"There's no 'of course' about it." Miss Berenson bristled as she came from behind the counter, "I'm not a mind reader, you know."

Meek as a lamb, Stubby followed the librarian to the card catalogue where he knew he'd be lectured to on the Dewey

207

Decimal System. I marveled at his sacrifice. But I didn't have long to contemplate. Erik gave me a shove and Luscious, too. In the time it takes to snap a twig, we were across the aisle and in the section marked, "Human Anatomy" again.

Luscious and I gave each other a congratulatory slap on the back, but Erik headed for the far end of the stack and started rifling through the books. He gestured that Luscious and I should do the same. The pair of us didn't have a clue about where to begin. Luscious fingered his way down the index page of one book then blinked over at me.

"What am I looking for?" he whispered. "Periods?"

"Naw, I think it's 'ministration' or something,"

"How do ya spell it?"

"I don't know! Do I have to tell you EVERYTHING?" I gave Luscious a shove to show my displeasure. He shoved back and I responded a second time, creating enough of a ruckus for Nancy Gunderson, the prettiest girl in our class, to peer round the corner. "What are you guys doing in the library?" She looked surprised, her violet eyes round as bicycle hoops.

Luscious dropped his book when he saw her. Nancy bent down to pick it up, scanning the title as she did -- *The Road to a Happy, Healthy Pregnancy*.

"What's this? Is your mom having another baby?"

"T-T-T-hat ain't mine," Luscious gaped in horror. "It fell off the shelf, so I was pickin' it up."

Like most females, Nancy knew a lie when she'd heard it. "You needn't pretend. I saw you holding it."

"I-I-I..." The accused stabbed his finger in Eric Ladde's

208

direction but Eric was nowhere in sight. Seconds later, the library door slammed shut. Luscious and I knew we'd been abandoned like yesterday's fish wrap.

Nancy continued to jab the book into Luscious' solar plexus. To escape, he pressed hard against the shelf so that the row began to tilt -- slightly at first, as if it'd been kissed by a breeze. But when the angle of inclination became too steep, the laws of physics took over. Luscious and I could see what was going to happen. We grabbed for the shelf but weren't quick enough. The row keeled over and slammed into a second, the one behind it. The second slammed into a third and the third into a fourth until, in less than a minute, every stack on our side of the room fell as if Luscious and I'd been playing a giant game of dominoes. Books and patrons went flying, as did 50 years of dust.

Needless to say, the noise was deafening. More ominous still was the silence that followed. One by one, people rose from their overturned chairs looking dazed, their hands groping for a lost pair of glasses or their canes or the book they'd been reading. A few straightened their garments, but most stood shaking their heads as if they had water trapped in their ears.

In the midst of the turmoil, Miss Berenson emerged from her place of safety behind the information desk. The pencils in her bun stuck out like porcupine quills and when she saw the wasteland that had been made of her Dewey Decimal System, she began to wail. "My books! My precious books!" I almost felt sorry for her; but then she clapped eyes on Luscious and me.

"You! You two are responsible for this!"

All I can remember after that is that Luscious and I were treated to some pretty rowdy language coming from a librarian. Of course we were required to clean up the mess -- which explains why I was home late for supper that night and why, on the question of girls and their periods, no one learned anything until Eric's brother came home on leave from the Navy.

Dad was late coming home, too. I'd just shut the front door when I heard his footsteps on the porch. He didn't even notice me as he rushed in. "Elsie," he shouted, shrugging off his overcoat and cap. "Elsie!"

The urgency in his voice brought Mom at the run, a potholder held in one hand. "What is it, John? Why are you late?" She looked worried.

"It's Mr. Papadopoulos. I found him lying face down in the street in front of Swanson's Hardware Store."

"Oh no! What happened? Was he sick?"

Dad shook his head, which made Mom fear the worst. "He-He's not dead, is he?"

"No, no. He was drunk. Out cold on the pavement."

Mom's free hand flew to her cheek. "Did you have to arrest him?"

I was curious myself. "Yeah, Dad, did ya run him in?"

Mom looked down and seemed to discover me for the first time. "Oliver Larson! Where have you been? Your brother had to set the table by himself. Go apologize and tell him you'll be doing the dishes alone this evening."

"Aw, Mom..."

She pointed to the kitchen. "Go!"

"Best to talk about this later," I heard her murmur to my father as I was leaving. "When there are no pitchers around with big ears!"

At supper, Dad said nothing about Mr. Papadopoulos. Uncle Henry was the one to raise the subject. Mom was carrying biscuits in from the kitchen at the time. "I hear you found Papadopoulos face down on Main Street, John. Drunk as a skunk they say. Did you arrest him?"

Uncle Henry flashed one of his lopsided grins, which usually set my dad's teeth on edge. That night, Dad didn't seem to mind, though. He took a biscuit from the wicker basket Mom handed him.

"Matter of fact, I did no such thing. I took him home. Figured that hangover's gonna be punishment enough."

Uncle Henry observed his sister's frown. "What's wrong, Elsie? Do ya think John should've thrown him in jail?"

Mom looked shocked. "Of course not! But you know," she nodded in Herman's and my direction, "little pitchers have big ears." Uncle Henry followed her gaze, then blinked as though sizing up his nephews for the first time. "By gosh, Elsie! These boys DO have big ears. Size of elephants'..."

Mom giggled. "Stop teasing, Henry. You know what I mean."

"Aw, don't be such a prude, girl. These boys know about 'demon liquor'. Don'tcha, lads?"

Mom squared her shoulders. "If you had children of your own, you'd know nothing good comes of..."

"But that's just it, Elsie. Something good has come out of it." Dad beamed at his wife, his eyes bright as agates. "Mr. Papadopoulos has offered free violin lessons."

"Free?" Mom shook her head. "But it wouldn't be honest, would it John? People might think it was a bribe. Besides, you know the boys have no interest in music. Remember the money

211

we wasted on piano lessons?"

I couldn't help nodding. My aversion to music studies began a couple of years before, when Harvey Erickson, the shortest kid in our class, had his near fatal accident with a tuba. He was on his way to his lesson when he tripped over Mr. Swanson's outdoor 4th of July display.

Mr. Swanson took his hardware seriously and had erected a pyramid of hammers and saws, nestled in a base of metal cans filled with whatnots. At the top of this construction, he'd placed an American flag and a sign that read, "CELEBRATE THE FOURTH OF JULY WITH NUTS AND OTHER ODD ASSORTMENTS."

Anyway, when he heard Harvey's yowls, the proprietor came running from his store. He failed to see the boy sprawled on the ground with the tuba stuck on his foot. The old man stumbled over him, clutching for the flag as he did, in a vain attempt to right himself. Sadly, the display that had taken Mr. Swanson hours to erect came tumbling down in seconds. After that, man and boy sat amidst the ruble, howling together.

A crowd soon gathered. Someone at the outer rim was heard to ask what happened. That's when Arthur Dimwitty, who was standing beside the passerby, shouted that he thought some street mimers were performing. People began to throw pennies and Harvey Erickson stopped yowling. Rumor had it he picked up fifty coppers that day.

Happily, my anxiety about the unwanted music lessons, proved to be unwarranted. Neither Herman nor I was the intended candidate. Dad was. And as Mr. Papadopoulos had made the suggestion without any promptings, Dad had decided to accept the offer. He'd always wanted to play an instrument, he told us, but his folks had been too poor to pay for lessons. Here was his chance.

"One day," he smiled, standing and putting an arm around Mom's waist, "I'd like to play a love song for my beautiful wife."

Three weeks after Dad's announcement, a package arrived. It contained a violin and a black carrying case. That evening Dad stood in the living room and drew the string across the bow for the first time, the way he'd seen Mr. Papadopoulos do it. The result was nothing like music, more like a cry for help. But if Dad was aware of his shortcomings, he refused to acknowledge them. And once the lessons began, he practiced faithfully, torturing his instrument, the family and his neighbors without an apology.

Over time, wisps of harmony began to take shape and even the trace of a tune. In time, Uncle Henry, who loved music, began sitting at the top of the stairs, his chin cupped in his hands as he listened to Dad play. Could it be that Mr. Papadopoulos was capable of miracles, we wondered.

November brought with it an early dusting of snow. I'd already entered the 7th grade and Mr. Papadopoulos would soon leave for his annual concert tour. Before he left, however, we would be faced with the fall recital. That's when Mr. Papadopoulos' pupils were called upon to perform before their doting parents.

No one in our family imagined that Dad was to be among the performers. If he'd have ordered a two piece bathing suit and said he was entering a beauty pageant, we couldn't have been more surprised. Worse, on the night of the performance, the night when my dad was going to humiliate himself by appearing with a bunch of kids, Mom insisted that we arrive at the school auditorium early so we could sit in the front row. We were going to be seen by everybody.

The hall filled up quickly. Little went on in our town after dark, or at any other time for that matter, so even the mayor showed up with his wife. My father was doomed!

213

Uncle Henry failed to see the seriousness of the situation. He sat, craning his neck in all directions, greeting people as if he were the evening's host. He didn't seem to realize that Dad was going to make a fool of himself. Maybe he didn't care.

After a time, the lights went down and an expectant rustle rippled through the hall as people settled into their seats. The darkness should have comforted me as I was no longer visible; but I kept worrying about my dad, a town hero, who was certain to embarrass himself and me.

Mrs. Pounder, Madison's piano teacher, was the first person on stage. She was a portly woman wearing a velvet maroon dress, the same she'd worn to recitals for the past five years. She seated herself before the Steinway to a flutter of applause. A brief silence fell, then Lucy Halverson, one of Herman's third grade classmates, teetered into the footlights. Her pink hair ribbon was large enough to threaten Mrs. Pounder's view of the audience, but the accompanist didn't seem to mind. She began her introduction while Lucy counted out the music bars by tapping the floor with the toe of her patent leather shoe. Finally, the violinist joined the pianist at the point of confluence and scraped out a shaky version of "Twinkle, Twinkle Little Star." Her performance so delighted her father that he continued his applause long after she had finished and the rest of the hall had fallen silent. He was still clapping as she walked off the stage, despite his wife's effort to get him to sit down.

Tubby Gunderson, Nancy Gunderson's six-year-old-brother, was next on the program. A pair of hands pushed him on stage where the bright lights and the blackness beyond seemed to make him forget his purpose. He stood mesmerized, his violin dangling at his side, and no amount of soothing whispers from Mrs. Pounder could get him to budge. Finally, his mother rushed down the aisle to add her encouragements from the orchestra pit. Her efforts set Tubby to wailing. He kept on wailing until Mr. Papadopoulos appeared and took him by the

214

hand to lead him off the stage. The young virtuoso got a round of applause anyway.

Mrs. Pounder looked relieved to see Dad next upon the proscenium. She gave him a nod, took a moment to adjust the score and then began the introduction to "Liebestraum". Confident that all would go well, her eyes never left her music until she neared the passage's end. Then she glanced up and gazed in horror to see my father wearing Tubby Gunderson's same glassy expression. The accompanist struck upon her keys as though upon an anvil. The gesture caused the back of her arms to flap but brought no remedy. The music died away and a silence followed that was perforated by coughs coming from the audience.

With little left to do, Mrs. Pounder began the introduction once more, this time playing with Wagnerian abandon. But when the last note fell, together with the last remnant vibration, the silence rushed forward again, engulfing my father, the piano teacher and everyone in the hall.

To say that a communal fear began to grip everyone in attendance was an understatement. The feeling was akin to that moment in "Phantom of the Opera," when the heroine reaches for the mask to expose her kidnapper's face. Everyone knows catastrophe will follow. No one wants to look; yet everyone does!

Amidst that silence, Uncle Henry began to stir. His hands flew to his throat and he made terrible, chocking noises as his eyes rolled back into his head. Mom leaped across me in an attempt to loosen her brother's tie, but Uncle Henry fell backwards into the aisle where he sprawled, writhing and moaning in earnest.

Two hundred necks swiveled in my uncle's direction; four hundred pair of eyes strained against the dark; yet none of those gawking individuals left his seat or thought to shout, "Is there a doctor in the house?" The paralysis that had afflicted Tubby

Gunderson and my father was now a general malaise.

"Help! Help!" I heard myself cry out at last. And that's when my father came to life. He sprang like a super hero, vaulting across the proscenium, over the footlights and high above the orchestra pit to land with precision at the side of his ailing in-law.

Tearing open the buttons of my uncle's shirt, he thumped hard against the man's bared chest. "Come on, Henry. Stay with me. You can make it! You can make it." And in the midst of all that pounding and thumping Uncle Henry did open his eyes and raise his head. "Take it easy, John. I ain't the one dying here. You were."

His wink signified that Uncle Henry had pulled off another of his famous pranks. The revelation gave my father apoplexy. Anger, panic, dread, each vied for expression until it seemed he might explode. And if I was close enough to see it, Uncle Henry was closer, which might explain his sudden recovery. My relative sprang to his feet and in a voice loud enough for everyone in the hall to hear, he cried, "I'm saved! I'm saved! John Larson is a hero! A hero, I tell ya!" The audience broke into applause, certain that what my uncle had said was true. John Larson was a hero. Hadn't he foiled a bank robbery once? Now he'd brought a man back to life. People began whistling and foot stomping as if they were at a tent revival and no gestures from my father, or the shaking of his head, could stem the tide of their good will. In the end, he was forced to endure shouts of congratulations and pats on the back as he led his family up the aisle for home.

Outside, once we were alone, Uncle Henry slung an arm across his brother-in-law's shoulder. "Cheer up, John. Aint' your fault I'm a fool. You did the right thing. That's what counts!"

Even in the dark, I could see the faint smile that played across my father's lips." You're no fool, Henry Westerlund. You never were."

The next day, Dad came home late and though it was a mild evening, his top coat was buttoned to his collar. "Where's Henry?" he whispered when he caught sight of me. I pointed to the living room and when he gave me a wink, I followed him to where he found his in-law asleep on the couch. For a moment the pair of us stood listening to my uncle's wheezing noises and then Dad coughed, loud enough to wake the sleeping man...

"W-what's up, John? Is supper ready?" Uncle Henry rubbed his eyes and started to rise, but my father shoved him down again.

"I got something for you," he said by way of explanation. Unbuttoning his coat far enough to reach inside, he pulled out a Labrador puppy, salmon colored and silky. Its first order of business was to pee all over my uncle.

"I guess she's marked you for her own," Dad laughed. Then he handed Uncle Henry the wriggly creature.

My uncle's eyes were full of wonder. "I-I don't know what to say, John. I just don't..."

"Nothing to say," Dad interrupted. "Only don't go giving her some stupid name like, Pomegranate." That said, he headed for the kitchen with me at his heels.

When Mom heard the news she gave Dad a hug, which left the back of his coat sticky with biscuit dough. She was wiping the coat clean when Herman burst into the room. "Dad! Mom! Uncle Henry's found hisself another animal! This time it's a puppy!"

Our father turned around to look at his youngest son. "That's right, Herman. And he's going to keep her." When Mom smiled in the affirmative, my little brother stared at me with eyebrows lifted. He seemed to be asking if these were our real parents or

217

pod people. I didn't know what to say. To understand, I guessed that he'd have to wait until he was older.

Epilogue

I glanced at my watch as I heard the front door open. Two hours had passed and I was turning the last page of mom's album when my father and brother entered the hallway. Reawakening to 1970 came as a jolt. I had lingered in the past for so long and so lovingly that I was still surrounded by its pleasant haze.

I picked up the collection of photos and carried them downstairs. My smile must have seemed out of place in that house shadowed in grief. Both men gazed up at me with a look of expectancy.

"We're home," said my brother, who had returned without a new snow shovel. "Things go okay?"

"I found this album from 1939," I replied. "Maybe, after supper, you'd like to take a look at it."

"1939? Was something special about that year?"

"That's the year you boys discovered Martians," Dad said, his memory as clear as if he'd been peering over my shoulder while I'd been turning the pages of the album. "You remember don'tcha? About those little green men?"

Herman nodded, thinking back. "I remember. I'd say that was a very good year."

"They all were." Dad stared down at his galoshes as the snow clinging to them formed puddles on the black and white tiles. If Mom were alive, she'd have shooed him out of doors or laid newspaper on the floor to catch the melt.

During the awkward silence, I helped Dad off with his coat. "How old is Ira?" I asked him, seemingly out of the blue.

"Ira? Ira Blackstone? Oh, I'd say he's older than me by about 8 or 9 years. Why?"

"I wonder if he'd consider selling the Yellow Banner."

"Selling it? What for? His kids take no interest in the business, it's true, but what would he do with himself? He's a widower... like me."

"Well, maybe he'd take on a partner then?"

Never one to enjoy a mystery, Dad spoke gruffly. "I don't see that it matters one way or the other. Why the interest?"

"I think I'd like to come home, Dad. Run my own newspaper, even if it is community news. In fact, so much the better."

Herman went bug-eyed. "Home? You mean, Ockley Green?"

"I don't mean San Francisco. Nancy and I have never been comfortable there. We're small town people. And I can't think of a better place for the girls to grow up."

"Neither can I," said Dad, warming up to the idea. "You and Nancy could have your old room upstairs and the girls could take over the attic... at least till you got yourselves settled. Why don't ya call Ira right now and see how he feels?"

"Hold on, Dad. I've got to talk to Nancy first and my editor. I can't pull up stakes over night."

Dad shook his head to indicate that he understood. "No, of course not. I'm getting way ahead of myself."

He looked so disappointed that I felt I had to give him some encouragement. "Look, I'll call Nancy and if she'll consider the idea, I'll talk to Ira tomorrow. You're right. There's no harm in seeing how the land lies."

Dad eyed me warily, not wanting the rug pulled out from under him a second time. "Of course it would be a change, a big change. What's behind this new notion of yours? You've never said anything about wanting to come home before. Is it this war? Are you running away? Because you can't, you know. We're all affected by it, even here. I wrote you that the Carlson's grandson was killed in Saigon last month."

"Yeah, I remember. No, I'm not running away. I'm running to something. And it isn't as sudden as it seems. I've been thinking about writing a book for some time, a book about life here at home. War makes it easy for people to be cynical. But we're not a cynical nation. Our country was founded on a belief in the rights of the individual and we keep tinkering with this democracy of ours to make sure everyone fits under the umbrella. That caring makes us people of the Heart Land, no matter what part of the country we live in or where we were born. I know this war we're fighting is the worst of times. That's why I've decided to come home. I want to write about the best that's in us."

Dad's eyes seemed to shine with approval as did my brother's, who at that moment resembled our mother more than I had remembered. I could almost imagine that she was in the room with us, cheering me on. I made a promise to myself not to disappoint her. I'd begin by honoring the spirit of this nation where it is best expressed, a place called Ockley Green.

About the Author

Caroline Miller is a woman of many distinctions. She writes short stories, plays, novels, and is a frequent blogger. _Heart Land: A Place Called Ockley Green_ is her first novel.

Miller's short story, _Under the Bridge and Beneath the Moon_ was dramatized for radio in Oregon and Washington. And her play, _Woman on the Scarlet Beast_, premiered in 2015 at the Post5Theatre in Portland, Oregon.

Her work is rooted in literature: strong character-driven storylines, descriptive imagery, and multi-layered meanings. She is a first-rate storyteller.

Caroline Miller was head of the Portland Federation of Teachers and is enshrined in Oregon's Labor Hall of Fame. She taught English in high school and at the university level. Ms. Miller holds degrees from Reed College and Northern Arizona University, where she graduated with honors in Literature.

Books by Caroline Miller

Caroline Miller's first book, _Heart Land_, is a fictional memoir of a boy growing up in rural Ohio between 1939 and 1940. During a time of social and historic importance that still resonates with Americans, Miller draws a humorous and sometimes poignant tone. The story is brilliantly driven by distant memories evoked from photographs found in an album as the family gathers for their mother's funeral during the height of the Vietnam War. _Heart Land_ is destined to be a true classic of American literature.

"... _Heart Land_ wears the triple crown of literary genius: it is profound, beautiful and arresting from the first page..."

> - _Writerface.com_

At the center of Caroline Miller's second novel, _Gothic Spring_, lives Victorine Ellsworth, an intelligent and beautiful Victorian girl. Because of her epilepsy, Victorine's maiden aunt deems her to be too fragile to attend school and Victorine is brought home to live under very strict rules.

Only the new vicar is allowed to visit the aunt and tutor Victorine. He is charismatic, mature, well educated, and interested in his young student, which turns Victorine's head. Her adolescent sexuality explodes as does her rebellion against the constraints of her life and times. Soon after, the vicar's wife has a fatal accident that shocks polite society, but does it have anything to do with Victorine - now a force to be reckoned with?

"..._Gothic Spring_'s main character, Victorine, is spoiled, polished, impotent, beautiful, cruel, intelligent and bursting with adolescent passion._

Her passion is the most compelling and tragic aspect of the novel. Miller's sophisticated observation of adolescent caged girls is profound.

I think Emily Brontë's sister, Charlotte, would say about <u>Gothic Spring</u>, *"Whether it is right or advisable to create characters like Victorine, I do not know. I scarcely think it is."*

- Dayna Hubenthal, author of <u>Persephone's Seeds</u>

Caroline Miller's third novel, <u>*Trompe l'Oeil*</u>, is set in France during the height of the French/Algerian war. It is a well-crafted tale of suspense set in a setting so lovely the sinister overtones and harrowing situations sneak up on the reader. The characters are a testament to the dark side of the author's imagination. Every story of Caroline Miller's is a surprise.

American scholar Rachel Farraday graduates with no prospects in sight. When she is offered a position to research a decaying chateau in France, she eagerly accepts. Upon arrival, she realizes the property is enveloped in mystery, including a honeycomb of underground tunnels her employer is reluctant to discuss. Her benefactress dies with no warning and Rachel inherits the place, gains a partner who may be insane and life-threatening intrigue follows.

"Ms. Miller is a powerful, eloquent writer." Silver Reviews

"Expect the unexpected." Good Reads

About the Cover Art

The cover photo (Title: *Children playing on sidewalk, the only available playground*) was obtained Courtesy of the Farm Security Administration - Office of War Information Black and White Negatives Collection (Library of Congress), LOT 1395, Reproduction #: LC-USF33-T01-000162-M5 (b&w film dup. neg., 70mm size) LC-USF3301-000162-M5 (b&w film dup. neg., 4x5 size) LC-DIG-fsa-8a00328 (digital file from original neg.); Carl Mydans, photographer

The back cover photo (Title: *Mailboxes, central Ohio*) was obtained Courtesy of the Farm Security Administration - Office of War Info Photograph (Overseas Picture Division) Collection (Library of Congress), LOT 1033, Reproduction #: LC-USF33-006644-M2 (b&w film nitrate neg.) LC-DIG-fsa-8a18763 (digital file from original neg.); Ben Shahn, photographer

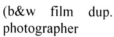

The interior picture based on this picture is titled: *Farm children on the way to school with lunch pails*, Courtesy of the Farm Security Administration - Office of War Information Photograph Collection (Library of Congress), Reproduction #: LC-USF33-T01-001230-M3 (b&w film dup. neg.) LC-DIG-fsa-8a03640; John Vachon, photographer

The interior picture based on this picture is titled: *Rear view of woman making biscuits in country kitchen*, Courtesy of the Farm Security Administration - Office of War Information Photograph (Misc. Items in High Demand) Collection (Library of Congress), LOT 9445, Reproduction #: LC-USZ62-92934 (b&w film copy neg.)

The interior picture is part of a picture titled: *Family who traveled by freight train*, Courtesy of the Farm Security Administration - Office of War Inform. Photograph (Overseas Picture Div.) Collection (Library of Congress), LOT 0302, Reproduction #: LC-USF34-020312-E (black & white film nitrate neg.) LC-DIG-fsa-8b34310;

Dorothea Lange, photographer

The interior picture based on this picture is titled: *Jersey cow at the Casa Grande Valley Farms*, Courtesy of the Farm Security Administration - Office of War Information Photograph (Overseas Picture Div.) Collection (Library of Congress), LOT 0649, Reproduction #: LC-USF34-036338-D (b&w film neg.); Russell Lee, photographer

The interior picture based on this picture is titled: *Poor children playing on sidewalk*, Courtesy of the Farm Security Administration - Office of War Information Photograph Collection (Library of Congress), LOT 1395, Reproduction Number: LC-USF33-T01-000116-M1; Carl Mydans, photographer

CPSIA information can be obtained
at www.ICGtesting.com
Printed in the USA
FSOW01n0450150615
7904FS